The Silent Heroines

Nada Lubay

Linellen Press
265 Boomerang Road
Oldbury, Western Australia
www.linellenpress.com.au

Dedication

This book is dedicated solely to the thousands of Grandparent-carers who selflessly look after and support their grandchildren. These grandparents are the glue that keeps families together, and our world is a much nicer place because those grandparents live in it.

Contents

Disclaimer

These short stories and anecdotes have been inspired by real-life events because you couldn't make it all up, even if you wanted to. However, to protect the privacy of the individuals involved, some of the characters, places, events and incidents have been fictionalised for dramatic purposes.

Acknowledgments

It takes a village to raise a child, but it took a whole lot more to write this book – far too many individuals to be named in person. However, without their support, assistance and encouragement, this book would never have come to life.

The author wishes to thank them all …

Prologue

When Donna took an early retirement, it was definitely with a heavy heart. Taking care of her granddaughter Isabella was a moral obligation she had no choice but to embrace. These new circumstances, to look after an infant child, became her most meaningful challenge in life. Yet the new, unexpected pathways of uncertainty gave her satisfaction and many rewards.

At first, Donna missed having daily contact with the professional people she had worked with; she'd had a busy career, which had kept her mentally stimulated. Giving up her job had imposed not only a financial loss but had also left her in an emotional void.

Before her retirement, Donna had a minimal view of the important role grandparents had in the community and society at large. She could never have imagined the struggles so many grandparents went through raising their grandchildren – sometimes even their great-grandchildren.

After retirement, one of Donna's first commitments was volunteering at the Day-Care Centre her infant granddaughter Isabella attended for playtime. Being involved as a committee member at Day Care, a non-profit organisation, gave her a new purpose and sense of direction.

Other social activities provided her with an opportunity to meet other grandparents in a similar predicament.

Donna always enjoyed being part of the community. It

gave her a great sense of satisfaction and enormous personal pride.

That role soon led to more engagement with other community events: PCYC gymnastics, Little Athletics, and dance clubs. When Isabella began pre-school, Donna started assisting other mums at sporting events and other fundraising activities.

Eventually, she joined the local Dog Club and the 55 plus Walking Group to keep her fit and healthy. There she met even more grandparents who officially or unofficially took care of their grandchildren. Getting to know so many grandparents who were raising their grandkids was a whole new experience – she realised she was not alone – they were everywhere: thousands of them in WA alone.

It was a real eye-opener.

Some of the Grandcarers she had the pleasure to meet were full of mischief and joy for living – flamboyant personalities, funny, engaging characters, all full of life – life was never dull.

These selfless grandparents, with bottomless love, had a sense of obligation and moral responsibility to protect and care for their grandchildren. They never felt sorry for themselves or complained about their predicaments – a resourceful bunch of old grannies whose spirit was, and still is, as strong as iron.

*****

Some grandparent carers also attended meetings hosted by *WANSLEA* in WA. This government-funded organisation informed grandparent carers how they could access other services or support systems available to them, as few were targeted to their particular situation. The organisation also offered some support for social gatherings, including family events, as well as providing occasional respite opportunities for exhausted grandparents. However, like so many other government-funded services, there was never enough funding to change grandparents' circumstances or reduce the financial burden they'd accepted when taking on the care of their grandchildren.

That meant grandparent carers often experienced increased vulnerability, especially poverty, when the social security system should have been taking greater care of them.

Other grandparents belonged to *Grandparents Raising Grandchildren WA Inc.* A 'grassroots' charity founded by grandparent carers, it provided them with the opportunity to get to know each other, establish friendships and socialise. Many grandparents with older kids branched off into smaller groups for social and emotional support. Socialising provided information on where to shop to get the best bargains, sharing costs when going on camps with their grandchildren and advising each other on how best to manage their circumstances.

However, some grandparents were disadvantaged financially and relied on charity for support and Food Banks to put a meal on the table to feed their grandkids.

At the end of the year, for Christmas, kids would get a small present and vouchers for school stationery, generously donated by businesses and not-for-profit organisations within the local community. These were always appreciated by the recipients, but it was never enough.

What grandparents needed was monetary aid and to be recognised and paid the same as 'Foster Parents'. However, the Federal Government wanted to sweep the grandparents' problems under the carpet. This is a Pandora's Box all governments were determined to keep tightly shut. It would take a miracle for any government to open it.

The more she got to know her new friends, the more she respected and admired their tenacity to survive on their measly, meagre pensions.

Many grandparents were scared of rocking the boat and jeopardising their Centrelink payment. They depended on social services. For so many, it was their only income. Grandparents knew nothing would ever change.

Unfortunately, many grandparents became disillusioned and untrusting of the system. Some were cautious, not comfortable speaking up publicly about their circumstances. They guarded their privacy and were not trusting enough to share their intimate stories with others. The social group members who shared similar life interests bonded together and developed friendships based on their personalities and circumstances.

The Grandcarers Donna met were a resilient bunch of people. They were tough and selfless oldies who had learned to survive on a shoestring budget, purchasing groceries at the Food Bank and clothing themselves from Salvo's shops. Like this, they somehow made ends meet. For their grandchildren, nothing was too much of a sacrifice. Making sure their grandchildren got school books, uniforms, birthday and Christmas presents, their grandkids' needs always came first.

Some of the Grandcarers Donna spoke with felt guilty, blaming themself and feeling shame in their parenting skills. That heavy burden sat on their shoulders, making them feel morally obligated to help raise their grandchildren. Some of these unfortunate, kind and caring grandparents continued to have daily conflicts with their adult children. Others were overly optimistic, believing and hoping their adult children would change their reckless ways and take over their rightful parental duties.

Unfortunately, this was nothing more than wishful thinking – unattainable dreams – for many Grandcarers. The waiting game often lasted decades, even a lifetime. Sadly, for some who were sick or had lost their partners, they had nothing to show for it. They felt disillusioned, unwanted and unappreciated by anybody.

Many grandparents were disappointed that the Family Court didn't view them as equal partners in resolving family matters. The system was, and is, geared to keep the biological parents as leading players in the child custody battles. DCP (Department of Child Protection) helped to build a bridge with biological parents by managing many grandparents and providing supportive parenting advice. However, in reality, the grandparents continued to have all the responsibility but hardly any authority.

The Family Court is still very reluctant to take children away from their biological parents. Grandparents are used simply as a temporary solution, applying a band-aid solution that creates uncertainties and even more conflict.

Dealing with their adult children's mental illness issues, drugs, and alcohol, is a never-ending, uphill battle, an ongoing life saga for many. They have so many sleepless nights worrying whether their grandkids will be safe when spending time with their biological parents. Most of the time, grandparents have to share parental rights with the biological parents.

When Donna and Tom found themselves in this same predicament as thousands of other grandparents, their lives turned upside down. Taking care of their infant granddaughter became their first priority and a major source of stress and uncertainty. Donna understood and empathised with those grandparents; she had heard many similar stories.

Would things ever change for Grandcarers?

Politicians and lawmakers should be made to answer that question.

*****

Wanting to learn how to better manage her own family situation, Donna started attending parenting classes to improve her rusty skills and to learn new modern methods of parenting. She wanted to learn how to cope when dealing with mental health issues; she wanted to learn how to better understand drugs and addictions, problems that significantly affected families in her communities. She attended free courses and short seminars to better understand how prevalent the problem was.

On one such day after the seminar at the University Campus, Donna realised that nothing much would ever change for grandparents. She had learned that grandparents faced many challenges in securing the income they needed to support the children in their care, dealing with legal issues, and accessing counselling services, education, and healthcare. This came from trying to rely on a pension that didn't consider dependents.

At least the grandchildren who lived with grandparents had better childhood memories by experiencing the feeling of safety and security and growing up in a loving home environment. Grandchildren had a sense of belonging, well-being and self-worth.

Sadly, the grandparents often struggled financially and emotionally, with no help from the government while keeping their grandchildren out of the foster-care system, thus bringing significant financial savings to the government and the community.

Research evidence reveals that children in kinship and grandparent care experience better health, education, stability, and security outcomes than children in foster care.

At one of the seminars Donna attended, she spoke with government officials conducting surveys and research on grandparents' issues. The statistics showed a growing necessity for grandparents to become the primary carers of their grandchildren, for whatever reason. The invisible epidemic of family breakdowns was sweeping Western society, which would change the landscape of childcare in a very profound and distressing way.

For many grandparents, their lives turned upside down in their effort to provide a safe home and happy childhood for their grandkids. They would continue to selflessly provide care and everlasting love for their grandchildren until their last breath.

Donna now fully understood the grandparents' plight, for she was now one of them.

Before the Beginning

Donna and Tom had a humble beginning: both emigrated in the early seventies, searching for a better life. Like many migrants, they worked hard all of their lives to achieve prosperity and financial security. Happily married, and after fifty years, they were still together and in love.

By advancing their education, successful careers followed, and so did a good life.

Donna emigrated to Australia when she was twenty-two years old. Tom, who was ten years older than her, emigrated a few years earlier. Two lonesome soles met 'down under', fell in love, married and had one son, Ricky. Tom and Donna had no other commitments nor dependents, as their adult son no longer lived with them. It was a time they could rightfully enjoy the fruits of their labour. They were excited by life and wished to hand down the valuable practice of work ethics and education to their sole heir, Ricky.

The only element missing in their adoptive country was not having any extended family members to offer a supportive shoulder to cry on. That was a considerable loss for Tom and Donna, especially around Christmas and other celebrations when families gathered together. Tom and Donna had to solely rely on one another, and that pushed them to be much more self-sufficient and resilient.

On a positive note, they made many life-long friends, were thankful for all their blessings and were grateful to be living in the best part of the world – in the lucky country – where they felt everything was possible.

Tom enjoyed a prosperous career, working as a chemical lab analyst in the mining industry. He retired earlier to appreciate the finer things of life – travel and having fun with his wife. But, Donna enjoyed her career and was not in a hurry to retire.

Donna worked all her life, building on her life skills and upgrading her qualifications. For the past twenty years, she worked as a lecturer in the vocational education sector at a Registered Training Organisation, assessing and overseeing students and apprentices at their workplaces. Her career gave her an enormous source of personal gratification and fulfilment. More than that, it gave her the social interaction she craved.

Donna and Tom frequently entertained. They attended cocktail parties, concerts and big-ticket shows, had a large circle of friends and travelled the world in style.

When their only son, Ricky, finally settled down with a beautiful Italian girl, everything was perfect. Tom and Donna welcomed Lucy and Emma, her twelve-year-old daughter from a previous relationship, with open arms into the family. That was the icing on the cake, an instant family.

Life was grand. A promising future was right at their doorstep. When they received the exciting news they would soon become grandparents, the beautiful jigsaw puzzle of Life was complete. No pieces missing.

Their precious granddaughter, Isabella, was born, bringing even more joy into their lives. She was a precious new life that, according to Donna, angels from heaven had brought to this earth. She was a gift from God and enriched all their lives beyond their wildest dreams.

*****

Soon after Isabella's birth, their lives came crumbling down. Ricky's and Lucy's mental health issues escalated out of control. Fuelled by alcohol and drugs, it soon escalated into domestic violence. The new parents couldn't properly care for their baby girl. Suddenly, Tom's and Donna's lives turned upside down, and they fell into the same boat as so many other grandparents. They had to protect this young, innocent child from the perils dysfunctional parents would impose upon her life.

For Donna and Tom, taking care of Isabella was an unfamiliar experience. It had been forty years since Donna had nursed a baby: her only son. So many things had changed. Parenting seemed much more complicated. Donna was determined to learn more …

One night after she'd put Isabella to bed, she stood for a few moments gazing down at her little 'Izzy' and the poodle-shitzu puppy curled up next to her. Bon-Bon's tiny body, her curly woollen fur as white as snow, blended in amongst all the other soft fluffy toys …

"What a wonderful sight … these two little angels peacefully sleeping together," she mused. Inwardly smiling, she suddenly felt overwhelmed by the beautiful peace and serenity, and she knew she should cherish every peaceful moment. Kids grow up so fast, and change would come soon enough …

Tippy toeing out of Isabella's room, she strolled to the lounge and sat down next to Tom. He turned to her and whispered in a low voice, "How is our little Sleeping

Beauty?"

Then he noticed the shadow of concern on Donna's face. "What's the matter, my love? You look a bit concerned?"

Donna looked at Tom and gently put her hand on his. "Oh, I am just wondering what memories Isabella will have about us as she grows up … about you and me … our family history, our cultural background, where we both came from."

Somewhat relieved, Tom replied, "We'll tell her these stories as she grows up the best we can. Why worry about this now?" His frown remained. "What else is bothering you?"

"Darling, it's more than that. How will I tell Isabella the truth about everything in her life, before and after her birth … how our past has become her present, which will ultimately shape her future long after we're gone."

Tom's lips pursed and he remained silent, absorbed in his thoughts.

So Donna continued: "As we get older, Tom, do you think Isabella will respect us? You may have overlooked the fact that we are approaching our golden years. Tom, we are getting older!"

"Speak for yourself," he laughed.

"Come on, Tom, be serious." She shot him a disapproving look, and he knew she meant what she'd said.

"You would be shocked how many grandparents I met at the Day-Care, at K-9 Club, at the Arts and Craft group — they are tirelessly and selflessly looking after their grandkids … they are struggling emotionally and financially, taking one day at a time, never complaining. I wonder when Isabella grows older, will she care about us or appreciate what we have done for her?"

Tom shot her one of his sceptical looks before giving his usual cynical response. "Stop kidding yourself. We don't really matter. Our responsibility is to ensure Isabella's healthy development. We've got a job to do … to provide a safe home for Isabella and give her an education. That's all we can do. The rest will be up to Isabella. Only she can decide which path she will take in life."

"But … … Tom, I feel so sorry for these poor elderly people. Now is their time to enjoy their life, and instead, they have to raise another generation of kids. The sad part is that these hard-working grandparents are unappreciated, and not valued. They are invisible."

"Yeah … the world now belongs to young."

"But without the grandparents, so many young people would never have had the chance of a better life. The valuable contributions these old people provide to the community and to society are taken for granted."

Donna activated her recliner chair to get more comfortable as Tom turned to her. "Well, my dear wife, most of us live in a bubble. In this new world, nobody really cares about older generations. We live in a world that is obsessed with youth – it's a materialistic world too.

"In that world, grandparents are not seen as that relevant. People are preoccupied with their jobs and families. They are far too busy to notice the outside world, especially the oldies like us."

Donna nodded slightly. "When I was younger, I was blind too – I was so absorbed with my career, I didn't know grandparents even existed. And I didn't care, as it didn't affect my life. When I was young, anybody over fifty was old …" Donna sighed.

"Yes, and the world is now moving much faster," Tom added. "Today's younger generation consider forty is old, and anybody sixty-plus is *really* old: dinosaurs. Like you and me, I suppose." He raised an eyebrow at her.

Donna picked up her drink and sighed again. "I agree with you. It's not fair to blame the younger generation. So many young parents are very dedicated to their children, definitely much more involved with them than we used to be. However, some of these younger parents can't cope with parental duties, for whatever reasons, and then grandparents come to the rescue. But, now that we are in the same situation, I appreciate grandparents' contributions in raising their grandkids."

"Yeah, I hear you …" Tom nodded. "… but such is life, my dear. I don't have huge expectations. It's been like that in past generations too. Nothing much will ever change."

"But it isn't fair. If it wasn't for these grandparents, there would be another lost generation. Having grandparents around taking care of the grandkids makes our world a much better place to live in.

"I must tell the world about grandparents' sacrifices. Maybe then someone might listen. Their voices need to be heard."

As if suddenly coming to a wise solution, Tom looked up and gave Donna a hopeful smile. "Why don't you write a book, my love? Do it for Isabella and for the grandparents."

Immediately, Donna felt intrigued. "A book? … Well … yes … that sounds like a perfect idea, but …?" Donna's doubt smothered her newfound idea. "But, Tom, don't be silly. English is my second language. I struggle writing school reports. I can't even contemplate writing an emotional letter; I don't have a creative bone in my body."

"Oh, stop this nonsense! Stop being so negative; it's not like you. I'm sure you will find a way. You always have. You are a fighter. Whatever you set your mind to do, you have done so far. That's why you were so successful at your work. So why stop now? This is just another hurdle to overcome. You can do it. I know you can."

"But, Tom, I must be realistic ..." Donna's shoulders slumped.

"Trust me, babe, once you start, you won't stop. I know you ... better than you think." He chuckled. "I should – I've lived with you for nearly fifty years. That should qualify me to know something about you, shouldn't it?

"If you take the same approach towards writing as you do to everything else, you'll be fine. The sooner you start, the better. As you said, we are getting older, so don't waste valuable time. Start writing now while you still remember," he laughed cheekily.

"But I don't know where to start."

Tom dismissively waved his hand and simply replied, "Start from the beginning, my love. Start from the very beginning ..."

*****

After Isabella started pre-school, Donna soon became bored. Spurred on by the idea of writing a book, she enrolled in a writer's course for beginners, purely as a hobby and as a way of making new friends. The course facilitator at MALA (*Mature Age Learning Association*) motivated and encouraged her to keep on writing, and she absorbed new writing skills like a sponge. Then she joined local writing groups, and The Society of Women Writers WA – whatever group she could find to absorb more information and hone her skills. And she kept on writing, most of it ending up in the shredding machine. She knew her limitations but persisted nevertheless. She just had to write her stories about the grandparents she met on her journey.

One day, many months later, Donna came home from one of her writing group seminars, laid her bag on the table and said, "Well, Tom, I think I am ready to write my *War and Peace*."

"So I will soon be living with a Pulitzer prize winner," Tom joked.

"Don't laugh," Donna said sternly. "I recently read Eleanor Roosevelt's biography, and one of her quotes stuck in my head. 'The only way to conquer your fear and to grow and prosper is to do something that you are most afraid to do.' I am going to do that, and the grandparents are my greatest inspiration to finish it."

"I'll believe it when I see you have written something," Tom jibed, calculatedly stirring her on.

With that remark, Donna's fear and determination rose.

One of her greatest wishes was that she could have attended primary school in Australia, to give her the basics of English that everybody else took for granted. She had emigrated when she was a young woman, and could never catch up on what she had missed; she wondered how to overcome that obstacle. And now that she was busy raising Isabella, her vocabulary had deteriorated from not mixing with academic women. She knew she would have to find the words somewhere and she would also have to learn more about using computers.

*****

Luckily, Donna had met so many grandparent carers who were happy to share their stories. Some stories were humorous, some were sarcastic, but none were ever dull. Some stories Donna had heard were shocking, but she so admired these hard-working grandparents, that she knew their voices must be heard. Above all, she wanted to create an awareness of the great sacrifices grandparents made for their children, grandchildren, and even their great-grandchildren. There were the hidden souls out there who were forgotten, and unrecognised, as they raised another generation. They were Grandcarers, a critical component that kept the family wheels turning in the right direction, in a safe direction when society's problems destroyed their family units.

The Grandparent-carers' battle is shared by thousands of others in similar circumstances, Donna wrote as she put her pen to paper, then outlined the content of her book, each story based loosely on facts she'd been told, and from first-hand experiences. Then she scribbled down a list, fabricating names to protect the privacy of the many individuals, characters, events, and places to protect their identities.

Miracles do happen, and *The Silent Heroines* story finally came alive.

Justice of the Peace

Just before the Family Court proceedings began to gain custody of Isabella, Donna needed some legal forms, witness statements, letters of support, financial disclosures and affidavits to be stamped by the local Justice of the Peace (JP). The JP office was in the central part of the city, at a civic court.

On that day, when Donna arrived, there was already a huge line of people waiting, most of them for family matters. Donna's appointment came in the late afternoon, the last on the list for that day. When Donna entered the room and closed the office door behind her, the JP looked up and politely offered her a seat. He was an elderly gent with a receding hairline; he was neatly groomed and wore a suit and tie.

"What are these documents?" the JP asked as he lifted his head. *He seems tired*, Donna thought. *It must have been a long day*. She looked straight across the table and responded, "These are my formal submission documents for the Family Court, affidavits and other legal documents that need to be verified before the due date. My husband and I are trying to protect our granddaughter."

The JP looked up as Donna laid the documents on his desk.

"Well, my lady, it looks to me you are well prepared and very organised. You seem to have all you need to start the process." His voice was strong and authoritative.

The JP had Donna sign one set of documents and then started turning the pages, stamping and initialising all the original papers, following the proper procedures and asking all the questions he needed to ask to ensure the documentation was correctly completed. Then he lifted his head again and looked up at her, making direct eye contact. His voice then softened.

"Good on you, lady. Fight for your granddaughter. Don't give up on her. These poor kids need to be saved from their parents. Oh, boy, I can tell you a few stories."

He paused for a moment as if to regroup his thoughts.

"I have met many grandparents coming to my office, and everybody has the same story to tell – drugs and mental illness are all around us. I see so many grandparents who look after their grandkids, just like you – don't worry, you are not alone. There are so many of you around. Nobody knows that, but I do because I see them often. Some come for me to verify documents showing they care for their grandchildren so they can get some measly financial help from the government. And they don't get much, I can tell you."

Then the JP's head lowered and he stopped stamping … "I wish that …"

He pulled his chair closer as if he wanted to whisper, but for a moment or two gathered his thoughts. Then, as if he had changed his mind, he frantically continued to routinely stamp and sign the next set of documents as if to distract his thoughts. But it didn't last, and Donna was surprised when he paused again, lowered his gaze and started to tell his story.

"Just last week, my daughter was hospitalised – she's still in hospital. It's not the first time, and it won't be the last. My wife is so stressed … beside herself with worry. She's at home taking care of our two grandkids." He drew in a deep breath.

"Our daughter struggles with mental illness; she started to self-medicate with cannabis. Her husband left her and the kids so we stepped in to look after our two grandkids."

He was on a roll now, Donna his last appointment for the day, so he didn't hurry. He had to talk to someone. He had to get it off his chest.

"Sadly, so many young people turn to drugs. Our daughter even stole some of her mother's jewellery and pawned it to buy these 'happy' pills."

He lifted his head and looked at her with sad eyes, and his shoulders slumped as he continued to sign and stamp her paperwork. Donna felt so sorry for the poor man; she wanted to walk behind his desk and give him a hug. But she stopped herself – he was a professional man and this was his office – giving him an enormous bear hug would be so inappropriate. But if she could have, she certainly would have.

The JP continued: "I wish we had taken our daughter and her no-good husband, who introduced her to the drugs in the first place, to the Family Court. He comes to see his kids now and then, and says that he loves them. But he has very unpredictable and violent behaviour. Who knows … when our daughter gets out of hospital, he may come knocking on our door once again and they will get back together.

"Nothing good will come out of that. We learned to cope with our situation the best we know how. And the poor kids are entangled in this messy game. My wife doesn't want to go to the Family Court as she's worried that our daughter will hate us for it and blame us for taking her kids away from her. The wife wants to preserve our privacy; she doesn't want neighbours to know about our family issues. She has always hoped that one day our daughter will change her lifestyle, if not for herself, then for her children. The vicious cycle continues. She is back in the hospital once again … until the next time."

Donna looked up, wanting to say something to soothe this poor man's mood, but the JP kept talking.

"It's such an enormous strain on families. Drugs and mental health issues are so prevalent in our community. There are many families with similar problems but because of the shame, it's hidden under the carpet – secrets that some families like to keep to themselves. I'm sure our neighbours know – they all feel sorry for us. They say nothing, but they can see when an ambulance or a police car arrives. They aren't blind. My poor wife is so distraught and worries about what will happen next … worries that our daughter may overdose by accident. That is our greatest fear."

Donna now felt slightly uncomfortable. This was so very close to home. When all the documents were signed and stamped, the JP rose, shook Donna's hand, and told her:

"Good on you, lady. I wish you the best of luck. Remember, don't give up on your granddaughter. Keep on fighting. Family Court will be a tough battle. Be persistent. It will cost you, but don't give up. Your granddaughter is lucky to have you. Grandparents are doing such a great job out there. I talk to so many in the same predicament. There are thousands of them around." He smiled thinly.

As Donna collected her paperwork, the JP sighed deeply again, regrouped his thoughts and stood tall. "It looks like you are my last client for today." He opened the door for her, his last words forever resonating:

"Remember, lady, the Family Law process will be full of surprises. But you stand your ground. Some parents should never have kids." Then he said goodbye.

As Donna drove home, she kept thinking about that conversation and remained surprised that the JP had told her such an intimate family story. His words echoed in her mind. *Maybe he felt that telling his story to a perfect stranger was a safe, emotional remedy.*

But his story inspired her. She remembered that conversation and the sadness in his eyes. Though she had only met him once, his story touched her heart. It gave her the courage and strength to fight for what was right. "Never give up on protecting your granddaughter. Fight to keep her safe." That was now Donna's only mission in life.

*****

Donna's thoughts drifted back to a time when she too had believed things might change. But she'd been wrong. *You can't change two people with core mental health issues. Mix that up with drugs and alcohol and you end up with a perfect storm.* She nodded to herself, for that is exactly how it had been with them.

Soon after Isabella was born, Ricky's and Lucy's relationship ended in bitterness and hatred for one another. Donna and Tom stepped in to protect Isabella when they realised that neither the mother nor the father was capable of caring for their baby daughter. Neither were managing their mental illness, and neither were coping well. The child was not safe …

Donna remembered the JP's words. He was right when he said, "The Family Court battle will not be easy."

Caring and providing a safe haven for baby Isabella on a full-time basis became an uphill battle, a never-ending struggle with the Family Court, and an emotional rollercoaster ride, causing her and Tom enormous stress and unexpected financial losses.

Their legal attempts for custody through the Family Court stretched for nearly five years, during which time they spent a small fortune on a lawyer who charged a phenomenal amount by the minute. Thinking back, Donna fumed that the money wasted would have been put to much better use, such as Isabella's education. She felt bitter: the biological parents, who were the whole root of the problem, were given free legal aid. Not a just world for grandparents, or anyone trying to rescue children from a dangerous situation. But how could that happen? That was the answer she was looking for.

*****

Right from the outset of the proceedings, it became apparent that Family Law favoured the biological parents, especially the mothers. No action was taken when the birth mother didn't comply with court orders; hearings were postponed when she didn't attend or didn't bother to respond to applications. Each postponed hearing still cost the parties lawyer's fees.

"Why don't the same rules apply to a biological mother?" Donna wanted to know, angry over the wasted expense. If the biological mother had been fined or even reprimanded, she would have been more observant of the Family Court's rules and regulations. Donna was angry over the wasted time and expense, but nobody listened.

In the meantime, Donna's private life was consumed by domestic issues, and ensuring Isabella had a happy childhood became an uphill battle. Donna and Tom believed Isabella, just like every other child, deserved to live in a safe and loving home environment. They didn't understand why the Family Court was working towards re-connecting the biological mother with her child. The mother didn't want to be connected, so why try so hard?

Tom and Donna naïvely believed in the rule of the law. They had faith that the law would be just for all. She soon realised how wrong they were. Seeing Family Law in black and white was not that simple – it had many shades of grey.

When the Family Court requested that all parties have their documentation stamped and signed for authenticity by the JP and submitted to the Court by the due dates – constantly emphasising that missing deadlines was not permitted – the grandparents complied with the rule, while the biological mother often didn't. In Donna's case, Isabella's biological mother, Lucy, with the help of her Legal Aid lawyer, submitted her official paperwork one year later, which was accepted at the Family Court, and nobody objected.

"But why?" Donna asked her lawyer, and she got her answer.

"You don't expect that the Family Court will take a child away from her mother, do you?"

Righteously, Donna and Tom believed that drugs were illegal so the law must be on their side. But it wasn't.

Then another shock came their way.

"You don't expect that all mothers should lose their kids just because they're on drugs, do you?"

"Of course, we do. Drugs are illegal, aren't they?" Tom replied, so sure of himself.

But he was wrong too.

Over the following few years, the Family Court, and that included the ICL (*Independent Children's lawyer*), desperately tried to engage the biological mother to be actively involved in the proceedings, any which way they could, practically dragging her in, kicking and screaming. When the mother was offered supervised contact to bond with her baby daughter, she came along, sometimes. The other times, she just didn't bother. The democratic system kept pushing the mother toward her daughter. Nothing ever worked. Everything was done to appease the biological mother – conferences, meetings, and countless negotiations to reach an amicable solution – but Lucy just wasn't interested: she preferred a lifestyle without parental responsibility.

When Tom and Donna complained, telling anyone who would listen that the mother was playing the 'mother game' just to get a single mother's payment and attending Family Court was nothing but a significant burden for her. Lucy wasn't interested – but still, nobody listened. They kept on pushing her. Then she quit attending altogether.

Nobody believed it when Tom and Donna told the

Family Court that Lucy had abandoned her child. It was so obvious – everybody could see it – but the system kept on pushing hard to reunite the mother with the child.

Donna didn't know it at the time, but it eventually became all too clear ….

The Family Court was a well-oiled machine. The system's function was to keep biological parents involved. Nobody wanted to see the reality of Lucy's state of mind or her addictions. Ricky had severe mental health problems too, and couldn't provide adequate care for his daughter either. That was also ignored. Mental health issues were considered too intrusive – a taboo subject that was too hot to handle.

But Donna and Tom persisted. They had to make sure their granddaughter had a safe and happy childhood. Putting up with the emotional rollercoaster, the many sacrifices and sleepless nights filled with worry was all part of the bigger picture. Desperately, they hoped the Family Court would be just, that grandparents could be equal partners in the raising of a happy child.

Dream on! Nothing could be so far from the truth, Donna realised.

Instead, the Family Law was slanted, and not toward the child and her safety. The pressure was put mainly on her and Tom to reach an amicable agreement. Isabella's lawyer, the ICL, even labelled them as too entrenched in their cultural beliefs, far too stubborn and unwilling to compromise.

But, Tom and Donna believed that Isabella's safety and happy childhood should override the biological parent's needs or wants. How come they couldn't they see that!

*****

In most cases, grandparents were *not* seen as equal partners, only as temporary solutions until the parents could take over again. Yet Donna and Tom naively believed that the law would be on their side, on the child's side, giving her a right to a safe and happy upbringing.

Their own lawyers had their agenda too. Money! Money made this more complicated than it should have been. Tom and Donna became frustrated navigating through that swamp of muddy waters. Nothing was crystal clear. Family Law was so flexible – stretch it *Any Which Way You Can*. For Tom and Donna, the Family Court experience became a very costly lesson. In hindsight, they could have achieved the same outcome if they'd represented themselves.

Eventually, after a nearly five-year tug-of-war, all the forces pulling toward the biological parents, all parties and their legal representatives came to an agreement. Consent Orders were put in place, agreed upon and signed. Instantly approved and stamped by the Family Court, it was a genuine victory, a win-win solution in their eyes. The ultimate aim was always to keep the biological parents engaged. This was paramount.

Even though Tom and Donna disagreed, nobody really cared. For them, there was no choice: they had to agree to share parental rights with Ricky, who was the second-best option, given that Lucy was out of the picture.

Predictably, soon after, it all came crashing down. Managing Ricky's mental health problems became an ongoing battle. Resolving conflicts daily became the norm. Would that ever change?

Never, Donna realised as she grew older and wiser. *It will only get harder.*

The Consent Orders stated Isabella would continue to live with Tom and Donna. Both parents were given equal access to spend time with their daughter. With prior consultation with grandparents, more time was available if they requested it. No other conditions were attached.

Sadly, Lucy, for her own reasons, abandoned her child. Her last contact with her baby daughter was when Isabella was one-year-old. Donna tried to reach out to her, offering friendship and goodwill, but the mother never responded and refused to have any contact.

Then Lucy's whereabouts became unknown, Donna soon realising that she didn't want to be found. Eventually, she stopped searching …

Donna also tried to build a bridge of reconciliation with Isabella's maternal grandmother, who lived in the same neighbourhood. She sent her photos of Isabella and visited her in person, hoping that seeing Isabella's photos would soften her heart. But it didn't. Sadly, Donna's desperate hope dwindled that Isabella's maternal relatives and half-sister Emma, who lived with her paternal grandparents in Pinjara, might want to re-connect with Isabella someday. When Emma celebrated her twenty-first birthday, Donna sent a card and photo of her little sister, but that only concreted a dead hope. All of Donna's efforts were ignored. Hatred and bitterness had blinded them to Isabella and turned their hearts to stone.

None of Isabella's maternal relatives, aunties, or grown-up cousins phoned or made any attempts to meet her.

Will that ever change? Donna thought repeatedly. *Only God knows the answer to that question.*

However, she continued to pray for it, for Isabella's sake. Maybe one day, these stubborn adults would recognise how wrong they'd been. All the time of missing out on knowing Izzy, who was such a beautiful little girl, was time lost that would never be retrieved.

Donna believed that every child is born innocent, and Isabella was nothing but a pawn in a dirty game of chess her parents played. Winning at all costs and scoring points against each other was all that concerned them, but in that process, the child's needs were forgotten. Getting even with their ex-partners was all that mattered, and this sustained their hatred and animosity towards one another.

When children get embroiled in the middle of bitter parental divorce proceedings, many end up as collateral damage, and often grandparents end up carrying the burden of raising the child. Parents who do this should feel guilty and ashamed of causing emotional harm to their children. Donna also firmly believed that it was the right of every child to have contact with family members and to be loved. To deprive a child of that human right is a sin. *In the end,* she decided, *only God's condemnation will relinquish their guilt — if they have any.*

Parenting Class

Parenting class started when Isabella, as a small toddler, started attending Day-Care. Here Donna met other grandparents in the same predicament as she. Like her, grandparents raised their grandchildren mostly because of a family crisis, and for some of them, their entire world had turned upside down.

Day-Care provided quality child care services and offered a range of courses for their staff for their professional development. Often, spaces were available in these courses and grandparents were invited to learn new skills in how to manage their mischievous grandchildren.

When a three-day course – *1-2-3 Magic Parenting* – was offered for free, several grandparents enthusiastically joined the group. The course aimed to teach parents/carers how to effectively stay in charge of disobedient children. Excitedly, grandparents expected this would be the magic wand they were looking for.

However, by the second day, some of the elderly ladies looked disillusioned. Gail was the first to start complaining. One of the most outspoken grandmothers, she was larger than life, which ensured the others listened to her. During the morning break, this easy-going, bubbly personality started whinging.

"Yesterday, when I got home, I tried to put into practice what we had learnt here. And boy did I make a fool of myself." She stirred her coffee aggressively. "I told my eight-year-old, Liam, 'Listen, boy, this is your warning number 1; you better go to bed. It's getting late.' But he just laughed. Then I said, 'This is your warning number 2'. Again nothing. He remained motionless and kept looking at me with that cheeky grin on his face. Then I said, 'Okay, I'll give you one last chance. This is 2½ before you get your final warning'. Then the little rascal jumped to his feet and jubilantly declared, 'Nana, you can't count: half is not a number. After 2 comes 3, ha, ha …'

"Oh, boy, I wished I could have used my wooden spoon right then. Like in the good old days … a smack on the bum did kids no harm. Back then, Liam would've been in bed after my first warning. No messing around with all this bullshit of magic counting."

A few giggles in the group confirmed their belief that counting 1-2-3 wasn't much magic when disciplining a naughty child.

Olivia backed Gail up. "Our facilitator is a young chick with no kids. She can't be more than twenty-three – she could easily be my granddaughter! What would she know about raising children? This course is a waste of time."

"I should've stayed home and done some work around the house," said another aged granny.

"Yeah," Olivia nodded. "I hate weeding the garden, but it would've been more fun than this. Besides, I ask you, where are these young mums today whose kids attend Day-Care? They should be here to learn how to bring up their spoiled little brats, too. No wonder they ask us to come to fill the class. Young mums dump their kids at Day-Care and go back home to bed. That's where I should have stayed this morning."

Florence stood up and looked at Gail. "You're right. There is nothing wrong with a good old-fashioned upbringing. A smack on the bum is all those naughty kids need; none of this 1-2-3 nonsense. In our younger days, I used a wooden spoon to discipline my kids, and they soon took notice and listened."

Aileen, a rational lady who hardly spoke a word all day, replied with slight sarcasm, "Look who's talking." She grinned impishly at Florence. "What bloody good did a wooden spoon do for you? Your daughter nicked off with her boyfriend and you got stuck looking after her kids!"

Donna had sensed some time back that some grandparents blamed themselves for their children's mental illness, drug and alcohol addiction. A heavy, unconscious emotional burden hung on their shoulders as they felt the shame of parenting their own children poorly. This was yet another reason – this sense of awful moral guilt – that compelled the grandparents like indentured servants to repeatedly rescue their children who got stranded in life.

Aileen, now quite agitated, said, "Listen, girls, it's not that bad. We might as well stay and learn something new. I, for one, intend to be here for the entire course."

"Come on, girls," Donna agreed. "Let's get back inside – only two more hours before a free lunch is served."

Aileen said to the facilitator during the session, "It's much easier with little kids, but I'm struggling to get my oldest granddaughter, Matilda, to go to school on time. She hates going to school because she gets bullied a lot. I don't know what to do about that? Matilda won't tell me what's wrong. Are we going to have some lessons on bullying?"

The young course facilitator responded: "Bullying is so prevalent these days, especially through social media, and some kids can be quite cruel. Time permitting, we may cover that topic tomorrow."

Others immediately became more animated and started bringing up their own problems with their grandkids, and the young facilitator suddenly seemed lost for words and couldn't get anyone's attention back on her 1-2-3 Magic session.

Gail started: "I can't talk to Liam. He's always on that damn phone or iPad. He can spend all day on Youtube. I don't know what he sees in that. He even uses his phone when we have dinner, too, and if I try to stop him or take his phone away, he gets so angry with me."

Olivia piped in: "When my grandkids spend weekends with their mum or dad, they come home so naughty and hard to manage. They seem to have less respect for me, treating me like an old fool. I wish they didn't go to their parents. It makes it so hard to bring up kids when parents interfere."

Andrea, the young facilitator, quiet until now, tried again to bring the group back to *1-2-3 Magic*, still to no avail.

Olivia grew more upset and tapped her water bottle on the table, demanding attention again.

"Family Law allows the parents to stay in charge of their kids' upbringing even though they live with me. I'm the one who's caring for them 24/7, and what do the parents do? They sporadically boss me around about their kids, and I do all the hard yakka. It's not fair, is it?"

She paused, then continued. "I find it very hard to talk to my oldest teenage granddaughter. She gets so bad-tempered and slams her bedroom door right in my face. She told me last week that she wants to live with her mum again. But I am so worried because her mum can't stay off the drugs."

Andrea then offered them all some practical solutions that could be implemented when dealing with bullying issues, her *1-2-3-Magic* session all but forgotten …

This was such an eye-opener for Donna: so many Grandcarers still holding onto the hope that their own children would change their reckless lifestyles, wishing that one day they would take back their parental duties and look after their own children. Most times, this was just wishful thinking, an unattainable dream, a waiting game that usually lasted decades or a lifetime. Some Grandcarers had nothing to show for growing older: they were always broke, living from one pension day to the next, feeling disillusioned, marginalised, and unloved.

Olivia desperately needed answers. She looked around the group for moral support. "My granddaughter never tells me anything. How can I help her when she doesn't respect me?"

Gail shrugged. "No good looking at me. Liam can be a real rascal and disrespectful, too, at times. I'm telling you, girls, computers and social media are to blame for everything. Parenting is confusing these days, and fuzzy. Who can tell what's right and what's wrong? Everyone has a novel idea about how to parent kids these days. When we were growing up, everybody knew who was the boss in the house. There was much more respect for the elderly, and kids listened more. Today, it's the other way around; adults seem to listen to the kids and what they want."

When afternoon tea was served, Gail and Olivia spoke

quietly together.

"Donna, I hope you won't mind … I won't turn up tomorrow. I have much better things to do than listen to this young chick telling me what to do," Gail said firmly.

"I would like to ask this young girl to come and live with me for 24 hours," Olivia butted in. "Then she can tell me how to run my life better. What would she know? She doesn't have a clue. Besides, she had no kids of her own – how could she understand what it takes to bring up kids … or tell us what to do? Hell, I'm on my second time around."

Donna realised some grandparents just weren't comfortable moving with the times but accepted them as they were. It wasn't up to her to lecture them on how to bring up their grandchildren, and Isabella was such an easy child. Yet she, too, faced many obstacles with her own adult son. Like them, taking care of a grandchild with no authority, support, or understanding from anyone only created a vicious cycle of conflict and resentment between them all. Grandchildren would always opt for the easy options regardless of how bad it was. And in so many cases, the grandparents were powerless to stop them.

At the end of the parenting classes, Gail asked: "So what did you think of today's session, Donna?"

"Well, I learned a few new things that I will try at home," she said. "Parenting is an ongoing struggle. We all learn as we go. When we fail, we just have to try different methods."

During the following months, Donna attended many more parenting classes and seminars. It was a valuable learning experience for her. Modern-day parenting methods made her realise how things had changed since she was parenting Ricky. She wanted to keep an open mind and be unafraid to move with the times.

One evening at home, when Isabella was asleep, Donna curled her legs up on the lounge to relax.

"Tom, I don't want Isabella to be ashamed of me – you know, being older than other parents are. Izzy may feel different from other kids. I think I should start mingling with younger mums … you know … I want to be a trendy, modern Nana."

"Darling, you can fix that real easy." Tom grinned. "Go to your hairdresser and hide your grey hair."

"You mean silver, not grey?" Donna quipped, one eyebrow rising in warning.

"Yeah, that's right. Then you will blend amongst these younger mums real easy. "Don't forget, babe," he added, "you must wear your old jeans and make some holes in them. Then you will be trendy just like the rest of them. It's a shame some of them can't afford new jeans." He chuckled at the thought of it.

"Don't be silly, Tom. That's the new fashion these days."

"I bet you these young mums are wearing the coolest holey designer jeans that probably cost a small fortune."

For Donna, though, that was no laughing matter. She knew she had to move with the times if she wanted to be the best parent her granddaughter deserved. After all, mixing with younger mums would keep her acting younger too. She wanted to drag Tom along with her, but he wasn't interested.

Soon she put her new attitude into practice. The sports carnival was on and she had to get prepared. She remembered last year's experience, and this time wore comfortable sneakers and faded worn-out stretch jeans for comfort – and, of course, she made an effort with her makeup to look good, just as she did on all of her other volunteering days, at Day-Care or PCYC.

At the school sports festival, she spent most of her time selling raffle tickets or cooking hundreds and hundreds of sausages, swearing afterwards she would never cook or eat another sausage in her life. At least not until next time …

While walking around the oval selling raffle tickets, she observed all those younger mums and wished she was sitting down with them. *What a life!* They were all sitting in comfortable beach chairs spreading food and drinks on a picnic blanket, relaxing in the shade in their designer-label jeans and sneakers. Now and then, one or two would suddenly jump up excitedly and cheer on their kids. And in the next moment, their heads would go down as they scrolled through their smartphones, frantically checking what they might have missed on Facebook. When their kids stopped taking part, some groups packed up their chairs and blankets and headed for home.

It was disappointing for Donna, seeing some mums leave early. Probably some of them were too busy to hang around until the whole competition was over.

Towards the end of the school sports carnival, one of the final running races scheduled was for parents. Donna was a golden age parent, so she started her preparations with slow stretching to warm up her old, tired muscles. She had to focus; she had to stay brave to race much fitter younger women. As long as she could complete that short race, that was all that mattered. *Besides,* she thought, *sports carnivals are supposed to be fun. Aren't they?*

Courageously, she started jumping up and down on her

toes as she reached the starting position.

"Take your marks, get set … Go!"

"Go! Go! Donna, Go! Come on, you can do it."

Donna could hear familiar grandparents' shrill voices cheering her on. She didn't want to disappoint them, and it made her run faster, and she overtook a runner to gain success. She finished second last but grinned widely at her effort – it was heaps of fun. Her best reward though was when Izzy came running, her little hands stretched out to embrace her.

"Nana! Nana, I am so proud of you."

Donna's heart sang with pride and joy as she thought, *Yeah, mixing with younger mums isn't so scary.* Donna was now one of them too – she belonged in two worlds, and that was okay.

Front-Page News

During Isabella's Day-Care attendance, Donna was elected to represent the parents' advisory committee, where she actively took part in various fundraising activities.

On one such occasion, a few weeks before the Federal election, the local Member of Parliament planned a visit to a Day-Care Centre to meet and greet parents and grandparents. A perfect time to secure a few extra votes.

Donna invited a few grandparents. This was the perfect opportunity to ask an MP why Federal Government had forgotten grandparents' needs: despite many individuals writing many letters and sending petitions to government departments and politicians over the years, no financial support had ever been forthcoming. The forgotten people could do more than just say hello with forced cheeriness but could speak with an MP about their problems of raising grandchildren: the MP could get it straight from the horse's mouth, so to speak.

As the selected participants gathered, the atmosphere grew slightly charged and filled with tension – the MP was running late.

Donna introduced Lynn and Penny from the Arts and Craft group, who she had also invited, to the group of elderly ladies, and was pleased that her colleague Tanya could attend too. She was not yet of retirement age, so didn't qualify for a senior pension or other family grants. Tanya had a sparkly personality and always beamed with confidence. Therefore, she was always at the forefront of conversations.

When the chatter died down, Penny took up talking about herself, never intimidated by the unfamiliar faces; she became animated, like a lively spark, re-igniting the buzz in the room.

To everyone's delight, Carolyn walked in smiling with a pot of tea and steaming hot pumpkin scones. As soon as the morning tea was served, the conversation grew livelier. Grandparents relaxed and shared their own personal stories.

Carolyn worked at the Day-Care Centre as a cook. She had superb skills in catering for kids with allergies, lactose tolerance and even cultural meals, Halal or vegetarian dishes. Under her watch, all the kids were well-fed.

Carolyn was a grandmother herself. Her grandson Shane attended the same Day-Care. When Donna first met Carolyn, the first impression that struck her was how immaculately groomed she was when she came to work. Her shoulder-length brown hair was neatly twisted into a bun, and her smooth face hardly showed any lines. She spoke in a soft voice, but her brown eyes never sparkled when she smiled.

As Tanya chomped on her second scone, topping it up with tons of fresh cream, she stared at Carolyn and wondered aloud: "Where do I know you from?" She simply couldn't remember where she'd met her. "I think I've seen you before, but I just can't remember where; it's killing me."

Carolyn looked at Tanya in silent wonder. After a long moment, she half-guessed what Tanya was referring to as she glanced at Tanya across the table. She stopped buttering her scone.

"I think you may have heard about our case a few years back. It is old news now, but back then, our story was splashed all over the newspaper. A front-page story," Carolyn said in a downcast voice.

Tanya looked at Carolyn again, and her mouth dropped open. "Now I remember. You are that grandmother …"

Before Tanya could finish her sentence, Carolyn nodded. "Yes, I am. It was my grandchild who drowned in the bath."

The room immediately fell silent. Everyone lost their appetite and stopped eating. The cups of tea were slowly and quietly put down on the table. The silence became awkward. No one knew what to do or say next.

Carolyn broke the silence. "His name was Jack. He was such a happy little toddler," she said, her face drawn, her eyes moistening as she spoke.

"What happened?" Tanya asked, then looked embarrassed, "but if you don't want to talk about it, that's okay…."

"Oh, now I don't mind," said Carolyn. She put her head down and gently wiped her eyes.

"My daughter Kate had two boys; the older boy, Shane, was five years old, from her previous relationship. Kate and her new partner, Rodney, had another baby boy, Jack, who had just turned two when he died."

Silence hit the room again like an instant fog as Carolyn kept telling her tale. "I will never forget Jack; he is always on my mind. I often wish for what else I could have done to save that poor little baby. I went to the police and all relevant government departments. I urged the child protection authorities to intervene; I pleaded with them to protect him. I didn't leave any stone unturned, but nobody took me seriously. The child protection authorities, to their credit, did eventually step in. Sadly, nothing was done to prevent this tragedy until it was too late."

Carolyn stopped and heaved in a deep breath.

"My daughter struggled with drug addiction. Kate would always come up with more empty promises. People who are on drugs learn to lie really well. She was so convincing. So, they believed her.

"I don't hate anyone anymore for what happened. I am past hating. I've moved on with my life. I just want to forget."

Everybody in the room was pleased that the local MP was running late as Carolyn's account continued.

"My daughter was so manipulative with everyone, including so-called professionals who should've known better. She promised she would stop taking illicit drugs and would go to rehab. She would do just about anything to keep the status quo. People on drugs are so crafty and street smart. Kate and her partner Rodney knew how to play the system.

"In retrospect, I now know that nothing was simple in my daughter's life. The events that led to the tragedy were difficult to control. Jack's father, Rodney, is a petty criminal, living on welfare, peddling drugs, and sponging on Kate's single mother's pension. Both parents continued living their reckless lifestyle of drugs and alcohol and having wild parties with Rodney's rough bikies and brutish mates."

"When my daughter attempted to rehabilitate her drug habits, Rodney would sabotage her efforts to go clean. He just didn't care. Kate was his slave, obeying his every wish for a daily fix."

"How come relevant authorities allowed them to keep the kids?" Penny cut in, unable to wait any longer.

"It was all known to the relevant authorities. I still wonder what difference I would've made if I had only tried harder. My daughter kept her life secret from me. She promised to attend some parenting classes and rehab, but she never lasted the full term. When I complained, I was labelled as the interfering grandmother. Rodney threatened to take a restraining order against me if I ever came to their place again. My hands were completely tied."

Shocked and horrified, as were the rest of them, Lynne asked, "Didn't the child protection authorities follow up on them?"

Carolyn's lips thinned, and she lowered her gaze to hide her tears and shook her head. "At first, the child protection authorities made one or two visits, followed up with a few phone calls and spoke to my daughter. DCP is so understaffed and cannot physically police every reported case.

"And talking on the phone, as you may gather, is like trying to attract someone's attention with soap bubbles floating in the air."

Lynne nodded. "You are right, Carolyn. There isn't enough funding to keep watch over so many abusive and violent families these days. Yet, so many kids who need to be protected continue to live with dysfunctional parents. So many unfortunate children are at risk of potential danger, but with few serious interventions, some kids are just lucky if they survive unharmed living with such crazy families. It takes multiple broken bones before anything is done."

Carolyn wiped her cheeks before she spoke again.

"Yes, some may be lucky, but my grandson Jack wasn't. He was such a sweet little boy. And he died because the child protection authorities didn't take me seriously enough. They didn't believe me, but instead accepted the empty promises of rehabilitation from hopeless drug addicts."

Carolyn put her head down and sipped her tea, her thoughts back on that very sad time.

Penny had more questions. "God knows how many kids are abused, either emotionally or sexually. We will never know. And you can't just blame the child protection authorities or the police. It's the system that's burdened with bureaucratic template solutions. If only someone would take grandparents' concerns seriously. Not to marginalise us, but to take notice of our lifelong experiences and knowledge. Grandparents know more about their children than anyone in those government departments."

Carolyn looked at Penny, pleased that she'd been heard. "You are so right, Penny. If only they had listened to me, my grandson might have been alive today. I was Jack's grandmother. I knew what was best for him." She gasped to catch her breath, to stay in control. "But no. The system ignored my concerns and took the biological mother's side and that of her druggy boyfriend. I blame the system that failed to protect my grandson. We can't fight the system," she said, her eyes filling with tears.

"So what happened later?" Penny asked.

"It was reported in the local paper," Carolyn whispered. "Quite a big fuss was made about that case. But, of course, like everything else, a few months later, the story was all but forgotten. It became old news, of no value to the public."

Donna remembered this case from the newspaper too and felt so sorry for her. And Carolyn was still grieving the loss of her grandchild. Donna could only imagine the pain she was still suffering. She asked, "Have the parents of the child been officially charged? Or accused of negligence for what they've done to this poor child?"

"Nobody got charged," Carolyn scoffed, looking ludicrous at the suggestion that someone would suffer the consequences of their actions. "The coroner's report stated that the child drowned accidentally, a tragedy for the young mother.

Kate was referred to a psychologist to address her mental health issues. Rodney was told to attend AA and an anger management course. Both parents attended a few sessions only, and that was it. My daughter continued living with her not-wonderful boyfriend. Nothing changed. Little Jack was all but forgotten … But I will never forget his sweet little face."

Her eyes moistened again, but she kept her composure.

Lynn looked at her, deeply saddened by her loss. "Yeah, biological parents, especially mothers, can literally get away with murder."

"Sad but true," Carolyn responded, but she still had more to tell. "You know, some people should never be parents. When Rodney got drunk, he turned into an absolute monster, a violent person. One day, my older grandson Shane made too much noise. He was crying because he had an ear infection. Rodney totally lost it and belted the poor kid black and blue. Shane's little face was so swollen that the poor little thing could hardly see. Thankfully, concerned neighbours intervened and Shane was rushed to a hospital."

Gwyneth also had two grandchildren in her care. She'd been quiet until now, but could not help herself. She asked in a strong South African accent, "That's horrible! Did you get any help from DCP this time?"

"Yes. To their credit, the child protection authorities stepped in immediately. I suppose they didn't want another front-page scandal. Shane was temporally placed into my care. Kate could visit him, but only under my supervision."

Sitting opposite Carolyn, Gwyneth reached over and gently squeezed her hand to comfort her.

"Well …" Carolyn continued, wiping her tears again. "I'm happy now."

"What happened?" the group of ladies asked.

"Rodney finally got fourteen years in jail."

"Thank God for that," they all said, almost in unison, Penny adding, "Finally, he got the punishment he deserved for what he did to those poor children."

"Oh, no, not so fast," Carolyn said. "That rotten bastard didn't get sentenced for negligence, physical and mental abuse, or for ruining my daughter's life. Rodney got fourteen years in jail because he was importing Ice and amphetamines into WA. He got arrested because he belonged to a drug syndicate and was busted by the Australian Federal Police. I hope to god that bloody bastard rots in prison," Carolyn said firmly. Then she clenched her fists. "In the end, that sad story had a somewhat bittersweet finish. On a positive note, there's one less drug pedlar around." Carolyn squeezed in a faint smile.

"What happened to Shane? Donna asked.

"Eventually, Family Court appointed me as Shane's legal guardian."

"That's great!" Gwyneth exclaimed. "How did you achieve that? We spent a small fortune on lawyers but couldn't get that. Fighting for sole parental rights for our oldest granddaughter was an uphill battle that we would never win. All that we heard is that we should be more flexible. Give the mother a chance to re-connect with her child. But it is not safe. We keep on telling them. But nobody is listening to grandparents. Why is that?"

Gwyneth shook her head, bewildered. Then Donna jumped in, impatient to tell her own story.

"Yeah. It is not just, is it? We fought for years, too. We spent small fortune on money-sucking lawyers and the best we got was 'consent order'. We also had not much choice. We had to settle on Consent Orders so we decided it is "better the devil you know than you don't, so to speak. When the biological mother abandoned her child we had no choice but to agree to share parental rights with Isabella's biological father — our son, who had been certified as mentally ill patient for over twenty years. It made no difference: consent orders gave him the authority to mess with our lives. I suppose until death do us part."

Donna's eyes dulled with pain when thinking of her son. She knew that no shine would ever come through those eyes again, but she smiled … and spoke convincingly, "You can't have rational conversation with mentally ill people. Unfortunately, Family Courts seem to think that grandparents have to put up with it. For us, it has been sheer nightmare, an ongoing struggle that will never end. We feel like puppets on the string. Keeping peace for sake of Isabella has been a monumental struggle. What can I say, we are too bloody old. Family Court decided that at least one biological parent must be engaged. Just in case, to fall back on if something happens to the grandparents. This is as simple as that.

"I ask you," she said to Carolyn, "why it has to be that way. Donna's voice trembled. "I want to know what was your secret strategy for getting full custody of your older grandson, Shane. Few grandparents ever get such luxury?"

"It's not really a secret. I got full custody of Shane by default."

"How come?" someone in the group asked.

Carolyn's face turned into a painful grimace as she remembered. "This was also reported in the local newspapers. This time it was on the back pages obituary when my daughter died from a drug overdose. Rodney was in prison and he was only Shane's stepdad and not his legal guardian. The Family Court had no alternative but to appoint me as Shane's permanent legal guardian." Carolyn gave a faint smile and a slight sparkle lit her eyes for the first time. "Ladies, don't kid yourself. I was told by one of my legal advisors that the Family Court will appoint a grandmother as a legal guardian of a grandchild only if the biological mother ends up in a body bag."

Carolyn stopped, and looked down before she spoke again. "In my case, my daughter and her baby boy both ended up in the body bags. I loved my daughter, but the drugs ruined her life. I would never get the legal rights of my grandson Shane if my daughter was still alive. All she had to do was say no and play the system by promising to get rehabilitated. For authorities, that seems to be enough. Please, ladies, don't misunderstand me, but I think Shane is better off without his parents."

"Of course, Shane is better off with you than with his mother," Lynn said sharply, supporting Carolyn.

But Carolyn waved her hands in protest. "It's not fair, is it? The parents have to die before grandparents are accepted as a viable and better option."

"But why is that?" Donna again, desperate for answers.

"Our government will never take the child away from the biological mother,' Carolyn repeated.

"But that's not right! The child's safety must come first!" protested Penny.

"Yeah, you would think so," Carolyn agreed.

"But Government is still recovering from the Stolen Generations stigma. With a recent historic national apology to the stolen children, Federal Government would never again be willing to separate mothers from their children. Regardless of the circumstances, the Family Law's aim is to keep children with their biological parents. That is the key objective," Carolyn stated with sorrowful resignation.

*****

Suddenly, welcome interruptions came along when Sally, the receptionist at the Day-Care, ran into the room with urgency in her voice.

"Ladies, get ready. The VIP guest is here."

Carolyn quickly rose and rushed to the kitchen to bring another pot of tea and a tray full of warm pumpkin scones.

As the MP arrived with his secretary close behind him, ladies greeted him with applause. Once they were seated, Carolyn politely offered each guest a cup of tea and pumpkin scones with strawberry and apricot jam topped with tons of fresh cream.

Introductions followed.

The next half an hour was spent in insignificant chit-chat. Nothing much resonated with the grandparents: it was all empty talk, with the MP constantly doling out the promises and pledges like candy to children. Photos were taken; a few handshakes. And the show was over.

For Donna, this was all a bit of déjà vu. She had heard similar promises many times before. Still, it was a very unsettling experience for so many unfortunate grandparents. No matter how well-intentioned their efforts towards saving their grandchildren might be, the story kept repeating itself, time and time again, like the cyclic sound coming out of a cracked vinyl record.

The grandparents didn't just struggle with the role-identity conflict as new substitute parents of their grandchildren, but also experienced social isolation, fewer financial resources, and less physical stamina than younger parents. On top of that, they had unexpected and growing health concerns.

Right now, the Grandcarers needed help and support from the Government. But who would champion their cause? Grandparents were so disillusioned because the system had failed them.

The Federal Government wanted to sweep the grandparents' problems under the carpet – push it out of sight and out of mind. Opening Pandora's Box was something the government didn't want to do. Keeping it shut down was much simpler. It seemed it would take a major miracle for any government to open it at all and lower the burden on the grandparents' strained shoulders.

Will grandparents ever get some genuine answers from the federal

MP to address their pressing financial dilemma, Donna wondered. She swept her gaze around the table. *Not really, because no one is fooled with this political curtain-raiser.*

And the only thing Carolyn got from the VIPs and MP was praise for her pumpkin scones, but conveniently forgetting the grandparents, who were the purpose of this meeting in the first place.

Donna had a bittersweet feeling that day, knowing that the price Carolyn paid to save her grandchild was far too high. She'd had to lose her daughter to save her grandchild, and she felt her pain. She and Tom had lost so much to save Isabella, but was it worth it?

Yes, it was. We saved Isabella, and the sacrifice is worth it. Donna knew that much …

As the day proceeded, when all the false formality ended, Donna speculated that Carolyn may end up again on the front page of the newspaper. This time Carolyn would be praised for her delicious pumpkin scones.

Nothing else mattered … When all else was forgotten, the pumpkin scones with tons of cream would resonate with everybody who attended, except the grandparents …

They would forever remember Carolyn's tragic story.

The K-9 Club

Donna joined a walking group to keep herself physically fit, and some walkers brought their little pooches. Here, Donna met many more grandparents who cared for their grandchildren, either officially or privately, and her admiration of grandparent carers was raised further. They were a resilient bunch, as Donna put it; a determined and selfless elderly group of Grandcarers, all struggling financially but somehow making ends meet even though they survived on a measly pension. Nothing was too much of a sacrifice for them to ensure their grandchildren received birthday and Christmas presents.

Every day, Donna took Bon-Bon to the local park for a walk, where she joined other dog owners for a chat while their dogs pulled and strained as far as the leash would allow. The park was open ground alongside a busy road, making it risky to let the dogs run loose.

When the local shire council sought public comment about different locations to build a safe enclosure for a new K-9 park, Donna immediately sprang into action. She collected all the regular dog owners' signatures on a petition for the K-9 enclosure to be built in their local park.

To everyone's delight, within a few months, the dog park was completed in their locality. It included a shaded shelter with seating, a drinking fountain – one for humans and one for pooches – a grassy spot and a sandpit for dogs to play and roll in. The local dog park quickly became a public attraction, a perfect place for dogs and their owners to meet and establish new friendships.

Over time, people became well acquainted, though they remembered dogs' names sooner than the owner's. It became a good meeting place for so many people who came from all walks of life – most of them grandmothers. Often during the school holidays, they would bring their grandchildren to run around with other kids and their dogs. Dogs barked, children screamed, and grownups chatted and laughed, turning the K-9 enclosure into something more like an amusement park.

Beryl was one grandparent Donna met regularly. She was a widow living alone with her teenage grandson. She never missed a day. Rain or shine, she'd walk in with her beloved old dog Ziggy, a playful Labrador with long, overgrown golden hair.

As the group grew to know each other better, some started staying for a few hours at a time, chatting about everything and nothing. Some grandparents started bringing chairs, snacks, and a thermos of hot coffee. Eventually, friendships blossomed further, and they began celebrating dogs' birthdays or other special occasions. Some grandparents organised family picnics, bringing everything except alcohol to the events. In a public park, alcohol was not allowed, but Donna thought one or two of them looked like they needed it.

Donna never heard Beryl complain about her situation at home and the reason she cared for her grandson; Beryl was always positive about everything. For her, a half-filled glass was always a glass-half-full rather than a glass-half-empty.

Her laughter and jokes would frequently have the group in stitches. She was an inspiration to all who came to the K-9 Park.

Some in the group wondered where she got her energy. Although she was overweight, she walked much faster than most seniors did. Even her poor dog Ziggy had trouble keeping up with 'fast marching Beryl'.

One day at the park, Beryl proudly showed the others a few photos of her grandson's football achievements.

"Ladies, look at my grandson. Mark won a medal for playing footy with his local team. Just look at this photo. Isn't he a handsome lad?

"He has his driver's license now, so I don't have to drive him to his football training. He loves his footy; it keeps him busy, unlike some of his high-school friends who are bored and turning to street life. Soon, he will complete his apprenticeship and leave home to search for employment.

"Oh, boy, that will be the time to celebrate. My boy is all grown up now."

"I bet you can't wait," someone in the group applauded.

"How do you manage? Driving a car is expensive," Anne asked.

Beryl sighed. "It was much easier when my husband was alive: he was bringing home good wages. Now things are much tougher. The same bills have to be paid but ... I always manage, somehow."

"Do you get any Government help?" someone else in the group asked.

"Are you kidding me?" Beryl's eyebrows shot up in shock. "Grandparents don't get much financial support from the government. I have to live on the measly old age pension as if I live alone. Grandparents get one payment of $400.00 per calendar year from the WA government. I am not that good at maths, but even I can tell you that works out to be one dollar per day."

Tanya looked up and nodded ruefully. "A group of us grandparents went to the Parliament House to lobby politicians. The WA government promised to increase that to $1,000 a year, but it is still only a 'one-of' payment …"

"Whoopee, what's that …? … just over $2.50 a day. Doesn't even buy the kids their school lunches. And the paperwork you have to do to prove we are legitimate carers … declaration forms and JP verifications. It's embarrassing what we have to do."

Anne nodded. "Yeah, I heard about that too. We may get it by Christmas." She smiled at what she could do with it.

"Yeah, I wonder which Christmas? Not this year, that's for sure," Beryl laughed. "It will probably happen just before the next elections. That's how things usually work, don't they?"

Amelia looked at Beryl, perplexed. "Beryl, how do you make ends meet?"

Amelia, just as curious, wanted to know: "It must be difficult raising teenagers. My husband, Joe, is still working, but we still struggle to manage on one wage. Beryl, how do you survive on the pension alone?"

Beryl gave her a stern, determined look. "I take one day at a time. I learned to economise by chasing food specials, and not wasting money on takeaways. Ziggy is getting old, and I have to take him to the Vet once a month to get his arthritis injection. I've got arthritis, too. I wish I could give Ziggy some of my pills. That would be much cheaper,"

Beryl said, then giggled.

"But he looks fit and healthy," someone commented.

"Zingy is twelve years old. And he's getting older, just like me."

"No way, Beryl – you will never get old," said Amelia.

"I'll be seventy next month. I will bring some cupcakes to celebrate my birthday."

Everybody had loved the rainbow icing cupcakes Beryl had made for Tanya's granddaughter, Sienna. The dogs ended up licking up the icing.

"Amelia, how many years has your grandson been living with you?" Tanya asked.

"We've raised Phillip since he was a toddler when his parents moved to NSW. My daughter Claire asked me to temporarily take care of him until their divorce proceedings were over. Since then, Claire has remarried and had two more kids, but she kept the kids this time."

"How long ago was that?" Tanya delved further.

"I stopped counting the years now. Phillip settled down in school and has many friends, so he stayed with us. He planned to go to NSW to celebrate his sixteenth birthday with his mum and siblings. But Covid-19 came and put a stop to that."

Amelia suddenly lurched out of her seat to restrain her little Jack Russell terrier. Jack wanted to play but was annoying Anne's lazy dachshund, Fat-boy, so-called as he was so obese his legs were hardly visible. Fat-boy was not in the mood to play.

Then Jack started chasing Bon-Bon. Both dogs were full of energy. Running around the K-9 enclosure at remarkable speed, amusing everyone, Bon-Bon's white coat looked like a snow flurry as she ran.

"How can you keep up with your Bon-Bon? She never stops running – her batteries are fully charged. Does she ever rest? She must be ADHD," Anne said, laughing. She lifted Fat-Boy onto her lap.

That remark set Tanya off. "Ladies, all this madness about ADHD! – it's far overrated. I heard some parents give their kids pills to curb their violent outbursts. If you ask me, this new medical labelling is just a good excuse to justify naughty kid's behaviours."

Beryl, as if stung by a bee, instantly looked sideways at Amelia. "Far too many kids are medicated. Kids and puppies are supposed to be naughty. It's all part of growing up, but that doesn't mean we must sedate them or turn them into lambs."

"Yeah. I wholeheartedly agree with you," Donna said. "Spending quality time with kids is all that is needed. Ladies, let me tell you, I love Bob-Bon just the way she is, silly, little puppy, hyperactive and impulsive … especially when chasing birds or postmen. Then she goes absolutely ballistic. If Bon-Bon has ADHD, I'd label her as *Active, Delightful, Happy Dog,* not *Attention Deficit Hyperactive Disorder.* That abbreviation is okay with me." She laughed as Bon-Bon started rolling madly in the sand.

The group sat smiling, fully amused by Bon-Bon's and Jack's play, their energy boundless till they stopped at the fountain for a quick drink. Then the chase started all over again.

During school breaks or long weekends, grandchildren came along to play with other kids and their dogs. On one such weekend, Donna took Isabella, who was now five to the K-9 Park to play.

As soon as they arrived, Isabella noticed her little friend Sienna playing with a puppy she hadn't seen before, wondering why Sienna's old dog Caesar was missing. So she asked: "Nana, how come Sienna got a brand new dog? Where is Caesar?"

Overhearing the question, Tanya, Sienna's grandmother, quickly rose to explain to Isabella. "Listen, sweetheart, Caesar died because he was old, and he is now in doggy heaven. Come, let's meet Sienna's new puppy. I'm sure Bon-Bon will like Suttee. Just look at how cute he is. Why don't you two girls play together?"

Having reassured the girls, Tanya returned to her seat.

But Izzy still seemed confused. She put her head down and moved closer to Donna, in need of a comforting word from her Nana. She whispered, "Nana, I don't want Bon-Bon to die. I love her so much. She is so cute," and she pressed her little puppy closer to her chest, not wanting to let her go.

"Don't worry, sweetie. Bon-Bon will not die. She is a young puppy and will live for a very long time."

Donna hugged her granddaughter and thought that this was the end of it. But, Izzy had more questions.

"Nana, I don't want another brand-new Nana. You are old too, just like Caesar. What will I do if you die? Who will take care of me?"

"Oh, no, my sweetie, don't you worry about that – Bon-Bon and I won't die for a long time. I am not that old yet."

That seemed to reassure the little girl, and soon, it was forgotten. The two girls resumed playing, leaving Donna amazed at how quickly kids recover; she watched the girls running around, cheerfully playing, chasing their puppies around the enclosure, seemingly without a worry in the world. But Izzy's words stayed in the back of her mind, and her mood became sombre.

On their way home, chatty Izzy had a few more comments on the earlier issues, making Donna realise Izzy had been dwelling on it but had figured it out by herself.

"Nana, I hope you die before Bon-Bon," the little girl said.

Donna was taken back, then she wanted to laugh, but held it back as Izzy appeared quite serious. "Why would you say such a silly thing, sweetie?"

"Nana, you told me that heaven is so far away. As far as the moon, all the way up in the sky. But if you die first, you will already be in heaven. If Bon-Bon gets lost, she won't be scared because you will find her."

Donna's smile settled back on her face, and she held Izzy's hand. *How logical her mind is,* she thought. *For kids, everything is so simple.* She responded cheerfully. "Don't worry, my sweetie-pie. Bon-Bon will be safe. We will always find each other. Nobody ever gets lost in heaven because grandparents are there to watch over them."

"When do old people die?" Isabella asked next.

"Only God knows that. But when that time comes, and that will take a very long time, Granddad and I will be waiting for you in heaven, too. But, sweetie, don't worry. That will take a long time."

"How long is that?" Isabella wanted to know.

"Your life has just begun. You are so young, and you will have many more birthdays to celebrate. Now, let's stop this silly talk. It is getting late; time for dinner. Your granddad must wonder where we are. Bon-Bon must be hungry too."

At a quick pace, they headed home.

That night when Donna put Izzy to bed, Bon-Bon jumped up and snuggled up next to Isabella, then she cuddled into Donna and licked the tears from her face. It felt so good.

Putting the dog back with her child, Donna quietly walked from the room, taking one quick glance back. *These are my two precious loves. Bon-Bon is still a young puppy, and we don't have to compete on who would live longer.* She felt optimistic that there would be many more birthday celebrations to come. Short or long life should be celebrated and lived as if it was the last day on earth. She still felt young at heart and was hopeful heaven would wait a while longer.

*****

Over the next few weeks, Beryl was absent from the dog park.

"What's happened to Beryl?" everyone asked.

No one knew.

Then one day, Ziggy was pushing at the gate, trying to open it.

"What happened, Beryl?" Donna asked. "We were all worried that you may have been sick, or something worse?"

"Oh, no, I wasn't sick. My old bomb of a car broke down. I had to wait for my pension day to fix it. Now I'll be broke till my next pension day. Luckily, I shop at the Food Bank and will manage somehow. Mind you, I say nothing to Mark, my grandson. He would be so embarrassed if he knew I had to rely on charities or Food Banks to put meals on the table.

"Kids don't care where the money or food comes from,

as long as their tummies are full. And that's good enough."

*****

One afternoon, when the others had gone home, Beryl and Donna took their dogs for a walk around the large lake. Beryl started talking.

"I hope, Donna, that you won't judge me too harshly. My grandson could never have things like all his mates. I could never afford it. I got so desperate recently that I did something terrible."

Donna stopped and looked at Beryl. "I know it is difficult for you. Teenagers can be very expensive. Don't worry, Beryl, you can tell me anything you want. I will never judge you."

Consoled and reassured, Beryl continued walking, and Donna followed.

"Mark's eighteenth birthday was coming up. I wanted to make him happy and prepare a small BBQ to celebrate that special occasion like other normal families. Mark was excited to invite some of his friends to his BBQ. However, I couldn't possibly feed all those young, hungry people. What was I to do?"

Donna kept listening, not wanting to interrupt her. Instead, she gently took hold of Beryl's hand to raise her spirits. It stopped Beryl's weepy moan as she looked up and saw kindness in Donna's eyes. Then she continued her story.

"I went to a supermarket and stole meat that I needed for Mark's birthday party," Beryl said. She glanced up to see if Donna was shocked. But Donna hid behind a straight face and kept walking.

"Oh, Donna, I feel so embarrassed. Imagine if I got caught stealing meat. What would Mark think? He would hate me forever. He despises his dad for choosing crime over him. His father is now in jail, while his mother is probably somewhere in Queensland."

Donna gave Beryl a caring hug, reassuring her, and Beryl laughed nervously. "Donna, I was petrified. Can you even imagine what would have happened if I'd got caught shoplifting? Mark would think that his granny would end up in jail just like his criminal dad."

"You must have been scared. Wow, how did you do it?" Donna said.

Beryl smiled shyly. "I was petrified, but I was on a mission. I went to the supermarket on a busy Saturday morning when it was extra busy. I figured, who would pay much attention to a fat old lady. I went for the most expensive cuts of meat. Nothing but the best for my Mark," said Beryl, as her face lit up with pride at the mention of her grandson.

"There were many people around. No one paid any attention to me, avoiding me as if I was contaminating their space."

"But how did you hide all that meat?" Donna couldn't help but ask. "It wasn't just a packet or two. You needed a lot of meat?"

With a silly laugh, Beryl timidly conceded the guilt. "I stuffed it down inside my pants."

"What …?" Donna grinned in surprise.

"I had big stretchy bloomers on. As I walked about the meat section, I would shove a few packets down the front of my knickers, just at the right moment. Walk a bit more, and then grab a few more cuts. I was so stressed. The sweat was pouring down my back while the cold meat was freezing my tummy. And yes, it helps to be overweight with the bulkiness of my body. No one could tell the difference."

Donna laughed. *This is more funny than serious,* she thought.

Now feeling calmer and unwound, Beryl went on. "When I came to the register to pay for my lettuce and tomatoes, I thought I may not make it. My hands were shaking uncontrollably. My heart was pounding like it wanted to jump out of my chest.

"Oh, my God, imagine if I'd fainted. The staff would have to call the ambulance to take me to the hospital? Paramedics would probably have ended up with a heart attack too. Plucking pieces of meat out of my tummy, fillet, porterhouses, and rump steaks, blood dripping all over my fat belly."

Now they both laughed.

"By the time I got home, my tummy was frozen solid. I'll never put myself through this terrible ordeal again. I bet you I lost a few kilos from the stress alone."

"And the party … how did it go?" Donna asked.

"Mark's eighteen birthday was a great success. He was so happy, cooking BBQ with prime cuts of steak for his friends. Nothing like he was used to before, eating cheap off-cuts."

"I made a few salads. Mark's mates brought some beer, and a few girls came along too. My Mark is such a handsome young man. He will break so many girls' hearts," Beryl said proudly.

"This year, he will finish his apprenticeship and go up north. This was his home, where he's lived all his life. I wanted him to remember his special birthday."

"Do you have any other kids, Beryl?" Donna asked.

"Yes, I have another daughter, Ashley. She's a good girl, married and lives in Albany. They own a large printing and office supply shop. Ashley used to do the book-keeping, but now she can't help much with the business."

"Why not?"

"Because the youngest boy, Noah, has autism; he's so demanding. It's so hard for poor Ashley. She gets so exhausted looking after her two boys. This Christmas, I will go down to Albany and spend a few weeks with them."

More than a few months passed, and Beryl had stopped coming to the dog park altogether. Anne, who lived in the same neighbourhood, informed the group about Beryl's recent developments.

"Mark finished his apprenticeship and accepted a job in Port Hedland. He brought a one-way ticket in his pocket and is creating a new life for himself. That's what young people do … then, when Ziggy died, Beryl sold her house and moved to Albany to help with grandchildren so her daughter could return to work. The proceeds of that sale would help keep their business afloat.

"They promised Beryl when the company picked up again, they would build her a granny flat at the back of their home. It looks like this was a win-win for everyone. Only time will tell," Anne concluded.

At the dog park, life went on as usual. The club members talked less about Beryl until they stopped talking about her altogether. *Sadly*, Donna thought, *life is like that*, but she hoped Beryl would be appreciated and loved. Her heart was as huge as her body.

*****

Now, the centre stage was taken by Anne, whose terrible predicament overshadowed all others. She had a son, Jeff, who suffered from mental health illness, depression, and anxieties. On top of all that, Jeff became a violent delinquent when drunk. Unable to hold a job or relationship, Jeff turned to drugs and petty crime. He was in and out of prison in a never-ending string of criminal charges.

Jeff had two kids from his previous marriage but had no contact with them. Then he found another girlfriend, Jessica, and they had another baby boy. Oliver was now five years old.

Oliver's mother, Jessica, couldn't stand Jeff's verbal and physical abuse, so one day she packed her bags and left. She never came back. She left her child, seeking refuge in obscurity from Jeff's brutality. When drunk, he turned into an absolute monster. Eventually, he was sent to prison again, and DCP appointed Anne as Oliver's primary carer.

When Jeff got out of jail, he could have contact with his son at his mother's place, but only under Anne's supervision. It all looked good on paper, but it was much more complicated than that in reality. As usually always is, it was a step away from a domestic nightmare.

"How are things with you, Anne?" Debby, who came to the park with her mobile Happy Dog Grooming van, asked.

"In the beginning, while Jeff was in prison, Oliver's mother would sometimes come to my place to see her son. But when Jeff was released from prison, she disappeared again. I don't think Oliver will see his mum too soon," Anne said to her attentive audience. "As long as Jeff is at home, Jessica will stay as far away from him as she can.

"Now that Jeff is out of the prison, he's moved back into my house and took over everything, including my little pension money. He never asks, and I never object because I am too scared Jeff will lash out and hit me. I witnessed what he did to poor Jessica. He's my son, but he's an animal. I wish he would get locked up forever.

"I just can't understand why women get involved with someone like him. Jeff found another girlfriend online while he was in prison. He drives my car without my permission, though he lost his driver's license for multiple drink-driving offences. But he doesn't care. He takes Oliver to his girlfriend's house, where they party on drugs and alcohol.

"He knows he can't do that – DCP was quite clear about the rules – but Jeff just doesn't care."

"How is Oliver coping with all this?" Debby asked, concerned about his welfare.

"Poor Oliver," Anne moaned, almost in a whisper. "When Jeff brings him back from his girlfriend's house, Oliver is so hungry and dirty. My biggest wish is that he doesn't live in the same house as me. I beg him not to, but he gets so mad at me for interfering in his life. Another day, he yelled at me and put his fist so close to my face and said, 'Oliver is *my* son, and I can do whatever I want with him. So back off you, silly old cow!'"

Donna looked at Anne, horrified. "Hasn't the prison reformed him in any way?"

"What's the point of going to jail?" Anne shrugged. "He spends time in prison, but it doesn't change him at all. He continues to live his reckless lifestyle, regardless of the consequences. That's who he is. I think the jail makes him worse. Sometimes I watch him pace around the house without purpose, acting as if he was still in his prison cell. It's scary, I tell you."

"Oliver is so lucky to have you, Anne," said Amelia.

"Oh, Ollie's so easy to look after. I love my little boy. Ollie gives me so much pleasure. I only wish that my son doesn't live in the same house as me. I always get so frightened when he's around. He shouts at me and I get so stressed I can't sleep.

"Another day, as usual, he took my car keys without asking and drove Ollie to the Aqua Jetty indoor swimming pool. Luckily, the lifeguard was on duty. He told Jeff that he couldn't let the boy in the water without mandatory swimming and flotation aids. When Jeff raised his voice at him, the security person bluntly told Jeff to leave or he would call the police."

"Did he call the Police?" someone asked.

"I wish to God he had," said Anne, then she sighed bitterly. "Jeff learnt this kind of behaviour from his abusive father. My kids watched him abuse me every day, mentally and physically. Restraining orders never worked, as the next time, his father was more violent than before. So I learned to stay quiet, and Jeff knows I won't do anything.

"When my oldest daughter turned eighteen, she moved out because she couldn't stand living in such a violent home. Jeff stayed, even as a teenager, and turned to drugs and crime. A few years ago, my husband died from sclerosis of the liver. I was so grateful that he's not around anymore to damage another generation of kids, but sadly Jeff has stepped into his father's shoes."

Everyone felt sorry for Anne. Donna was appalled. What a scary prospect it was: letting a five-year-old in a car with a man with no license and who was probably drunk. But who was watching? *Poor Anne. She is doing her best to look after this little boy under such difficult circumstances.*

Sadly for Anne, she, just like thousands of other grandparents, was a prisoner of her moral obligations. For how long would Anne be able to take care of two different generations? – her criminal alcoholic son and her little baby grandson? Would she last the distance? Or would she die from stress-related illness or sheer exhaustion? Or, God forbid, in extreme cases, would she die a violent death at the hands of her own son?

A few months later, Anne came to the dog club smiling broadly. Before anyone could speak, an overjoyed Anne said that she'd been given a reprieve from fear and stress.

"Jeff got into trouble with the law again and is now behind bars."

"That's splendid news," said Trudy, a stout but attractive grandparent who was dressed in flashy, gypsy-coloured clothing.

"Let's hope the bastard stays locked up for a long time."

"Yes," said Anne laughingly. "He assaulted a police officer, so this time he'll be locked up for much longer. Nobody assaults the police and gets away with it. I feel sorry for that police officer but grateful that God must have answered my prayers. Ollie and I will now sleep much better. And who knows … maybe Ollie's mum will come and visit her little boy again."

A sparkle they hadn't seen for a very long time was back in Anne's eyes. The K9 group was so happy for her – she suffered so much; it was time for her to have some peace.

Donna was delighted to hear Anne's good news, but her thoughts drifted elsewhere as she moved away with an excuse to see what Bon-Bon was up to. She gazed into the distance, wanting to push her tormented thoughts from her head, but couldn't.

Donna's life was similar to Anne's, but Anne was lucky that her son Jeff was sent to prison. For Anne, this was immediate newfound freedom, liberation, fresh air to breathe, and a clean home to enjoy. But for Donna, there was no such luck. Her son had an incurable illness – a mental disability. He could never be locked up. Mental health departments didn't have enough beds or enough staff to adequately manage mental health. It was an immense problem and now, with Covid-19, it would only get worse.

Donna was a prisoner, too. She could never be unchained from being entangled with her son's mental demons. She had battled all of her life to escape her son's madness, his endless negative energy and destructive behaviour. The nightmare would never end, but Donna still desperately searched for answers. So far, she had never found them. She had to manage her own son's madness and somehow preserve her own sanity. And she had the responsibility to provide a stable and happy childhood for her granddaughter, Izzy …

*****

When Donna sat down with Bon-Bon in her lap, Trudy

started talking with Anne. She was so boisterous and not bothered who listened in. Looking at Trudy, Donna couldn't help a sneaky grin crossing her face.

Trudy was the youngest in the dog group and lived like a hippy. She was overweight for her small stature, but she dressed trendy and kept her appearance youthful. Her short butch-looking hair had dark red and purple streaks through it, and her body was decorated with tattoos, which she loved to show off.

Never one to mince words, Trudy came across as confident and self-opinionated. This time she talked about her daughter, Megan, and her six-year-old granddaughter, Daisy, who had lived with her since she was born.

"My daughter Megan is addicted to drugs. She is sick."

"Sorry to hear that your daughter is a junkie," Beverly, one of the new grandparents that joined only recently, blurted out. She had two little Chihuahuas and made no allowances for decorum.

Looking suddenly cross and unfriendly, Trudy gave Beverly a sharp, contemptuous glare. "I get so irritated with people like you who won't recognise that drug addiction is an illness. Because it bloody is. You are just too narrow-minded to see it."

Everyone went silent, unsure of what had just happened.

"Ooh … don't get so touchy, Trudy. I meant no offence," Beverly retorted, now very uncomfortable and unhappy.

"My daughter is in poor health," continued Trudy, looking straight at Beverly but actually addressing the entire group. "Megan is ill from using drugs as a way of coping with many pressures in her life. Her bastard boyfriend left her, and she lost her job."

"I'm sorry," said Beverly in a subdued tone.

Trudy seemed mollified. The buzz of conversation slowly resumed. Rhonda, dressed in a worn-out tracksuit full of dog hair from her Yorkshire terrier dog, Rosie, rolled her eyes and whispered something to Debby, who sat next to her.

Debby had come a few times now, but often with a different dog – she had rescued so many abandoned dogs. She owned a Happy Dog Grooming business and generously offered a discount to the K-9 group. After her son's messy divorce, her granddaughter moved in with her. Young Heather helped her with her grooming business, and Debby, in return, had paid her university fees. Heather was now a qualified vet working in a large veterinary hospital. The K-9 group also got discounted fees when they brought their dogs to her veterinary surgery.

Rhonda and Debby both strongly disagreed with Trudy's statement, Rhonda being quite vocal about it. She told Debby that addiction was not an illness, but a lifestyle choice.

Luckily they stood further away, so their remarks went unheard, and Trudy missed what the girls had said. Otherwise, they would have copped it from Trudy's sharp tongue.

Unsure if some of the group were still in any doubt, Trudy repeated slowly: "My daughter is ill because drug addiction is an illness. You should see my poor girl's arms … black and blue from needle punctures. She hides it by wearing long-sleeved shirts, even on the hottest summer days. Now, don't tell me that this is not an illness? Megan is sick and needs a doctor. She has to rehabilitate her habits, that's all."

Donna asked in a cheery voice to steer the conversation away from the contentious subject of illicit drugs. "Trudy, you have a little granddaughter, don't you?"

"Yes, I do. Daisy is such a lovely little girl. I am so lucky she has no serious illness, as her mother used drugs while she was pregnant. Daisy was born prematurely, with drugs in her body. Poor little thing … she spent weeks in intensive care. It was touch and go for a while. But I am so happy she is now a healthy little girl. I've just enrolled Daisy in ballet classes; she loves to perform. She's my little princess."

Trudy had been appointed by DCP, the child protection authorities, to be Megan's supervisor, to monitor her behaviour and help her with her drug rehabilitation. The problem was that Megan, as Daisy's biological mother, had kept all the parental rights to the child. Trudy had no choice but to accept being her granddaughter's supervisor. Like so many other Grandcarers, Trudy had to take one day at a time.

Technically, her druggie daughter was to make all the legal decisions for Daisy. With the child protection authorities not having the human resources to police all their cases, Trudy had to learn how to resolve conflict with her daughter and protect her granddaughter. Like so many other grandparents dealing with their kids' drug addictions, taking one step forward and often two steps back.

Trudy told the K-9 group, "I'm so pleased that Megan is on a pill now so she won't have any more unplanned pregnancies."

"So, where is Megan now?" Donna asked.

"I don't know … She comes and goes as she pleases." Trudy's low voice trailed off into silence.

"But Daisy is still with you, right?" Donna asked in a quiet but worried voice.

"Yes," Trudy said, her hands nervously wringing and shaking. "I get so stressed when Megan takes Daisy away to her new boyfriend's place. I can't sleep for continually worrying about what could happen to a little girl in a drug-infested house with all those blokes, drinking, smoking, snorting, laughing, and fooling around.

"When Megan was on heavy drugs, she was a full-blown addict and was always spaced out. Most of the time, she didn't know what was happening around her. Oh, God, I can't think about it. It gives me the shivers."

Donna quickly put her arm around Trudy's shoulders to calm her while everyone else in the group stopped talking again.

"Why can't you seek a sole custody order from the Court?" Anne asked.

"Megan is not willing to sign the consent order. Why would she? She gets more money as a single mother than I do as a pensioner. And the Court is constrained by the Family Law Act 1975 not to take parental responsibility from the parents. I need excellent lawyers to challenge that – even if there is a good reason for that – but I don't have that kind of money."

"This must be so hard for you," said Amelia.

"Yes, it is. I agreed to help to look after my little Daisy. When Megan gets high, she is so unreasonable. I tried everything, but I just couldn't stop her from using drugs.

"Megan is sick. It's sickness, you know. She tried to give

up so many times, but her rehabilitations never ever worked. She would stay clean for a few months, and then the rollercoaster ride would start all over again. I never wanted to be a full-time parent, but what choice do I have?"

Trudy sighed and looked around the group. "The system is faulty. They will try absolutely everything to help the biological mother. We, the Grandcarers, are mainly considered as temporary carers. We are too bloody old to be long-term carers. In our society, the grandparents are expendable ... sacrifices for a greater cause – for the younger generation, for our grandchildren."

After pausing for a moment, Trudy opened the floodgates of her calamity. "When Megan is spaced out, she never knows who or where she is. She forgets she is a mum, or that she has a child that needs looking after. As long as Daisy has a roof over her head, that's all she cares about. But who is looking after Daisy when Megan is stoned? In all but name, I am Daisy's mum, that's who! Megan is now attending rehabilitation sessions seriously and only smokes cannabis. That calms her down."

She shook her head again. "Megan stays away from home for most of the week, partying and having fun. She comes home only to shower or grab some clothes or when she needs something; money mainly. One weekend, Megan was in horrible shape. She had such horrible withdrawals from the lack of a fix. So Megan went to her boyfriend's house to get some. But she also wanted to take Daisy with her. When I objected, Megan hysterically yelled back at me. 'You can't stop me! I am Daisy's mother. She is my baby girl. I miss her when she is not with me. Daisy is mine, not yours. Mine! Do you hear me!'."

Choking back her tears, Trudy continued. "Another day, she came to me and said, 'if you give me $100, I'll let you keep Daisy while I'm away'."

Everyone in the group was now astonished; their jaws dropped wide open, more in disgust than surprise. Then Trudy's lament turned to anger.

"I said to her, I don't have $100. I am struggling this week. Then Megan asked, well, how much do you have? I said I only had $50, and I showed her my purse to prove it. I told her that this must last me until my next pension, but Megan just said, 'Okay, that will do' and she grabbed the money and ran outside to her car. It looked like someone was sitting inside the car, waiting for her."

A few months later, Donna bumped into Trudy at the local shopping centre, and they went for lunch and a glass of wine to the foreshore restaurant. After a few extra glasses of wine, Trudy had so much more to tell.

"Yesterday, Megan gave me another nasty surprise. She said that someone called Darren may see Daisy because he is her father. But I know better than that. Megan actually does not know who Daisy's father is. She was too stoned at the time of conception – she told me that herself. And I know she would sell her body to a devil or the highest bidder for good dope. She changes her boyfriends like her underwear and has a quickie with anybody who can provide her with her next fix."

Trudy sighed mournfully, this time with resigned acceptance. "I still consider myself lucky that my daughter and granddaughter still live with me under the same roof. If it wasn't for me, Megan would end up sleeping under a bridge … or worse, she would be dead by now. She is sick and headstrong, just the way her father was.

"When Megan turned to drugs, he felt devastated and helpless, seeing his only daughter sinking into a black hole. He couldn't cope with living like that, so he walked out on both of us. We eventually got divorced." She wiped away a tear that rolled down her cheek.

"Bloody drugs, they are everywhere these days. Donna, I'm telling you, I gave Megan the best years of my life. And now, it gets so lonely … I miss having a man in my life."

Donna nodded with understanding. "Trudy, you are still young and attractive. You are one spunky looking lady." She half-smiled, trying to cheer her up.

"Yeah, Donna, thanks. But who wants to be with a woman like me with all my problems. That's why my husband left me. The issues are just too big. None of our families wants anything to do with Megan and me anymore. They have all abandoned us like trash.

"And there's more," Trudy said with sad resignation. "You better hold on to your chair … Megan is pregnant again."

Donna tried to suppress a grimace but couldn't. "But you told me she was on the pill!"

"Well, obviously not. Megan used to take so many amphetamines that she must've got them mixed up."

"What now?" Donna asked.

Trudy took a long sip of her third glass of wine. Donna, still nursing her first glass, pretended not to notice Trudy's thirst.

"I'll have to prepare for another mouth to feed. What option do I have? Megan is my only child, and I love her. I know she is trying to give up drugs. She just can't. It's difficult to see your child practically dying before your eyes. I must do everything to save my daughter and her babies."

Donna rose and paid for lunch. Walking out of the restaurant into a refreshing sea breeze, recovered their sagging spirits a little. They stopped for ice cream and sat on the boardwalk bench as Trudy continued to chat about a new baby.

Then Trudy gave Donna a hug. "It is so good to talk to somebody who understands and doesn't judge. You gave me all that I needed, a few kind words of empathy and understanding."

Donna nodded to reassure her.

But Trudy was still chatty and obviously not in a hurry. She wanted to wait to catch a later bus as all that wine had made her a little tipsy.

"Come on, Donna, let's go across the road and get a cappuccino?

When they had settled in the coffee shop, Trudy continued her story. "We grandparents are all in the same boat. That's why we need to help and support each other, my dear. Without each other, we are on our own.

"Megan is now attending rehabilitation sessions seriously and only smokes cannabis. That calms her down. When I am all alone at home, my only staunch friend is my dog."

"He is a lovely dog, so gentle, but why have you named him Copper?" Donna wanted to know.

"Megan named him Copper from the slang term 'cop' because he can sniff drugs much better than the police can. Copper used to work at the airports as a sniffer dog, screening airport passengers. When I saw an advertisement that some of those Beagles were being retired and offered for sale, I bought one."

"Why a sniffer dog, as cute as they are?"

"When Megan agreed to attend rehabilitation, Copper helped me keep Megan clean. He has such an incredible sense of smell. He can detect if Megan used any heavy drugs. If she did, the dog would react as trained, and I would know at once that she had faltered in her rehabilitation. An intelligent dog, eh? Mind you, Copper was worth every penny I paid for him.

"Every time Megan would come home, Copper would go nuts, all the red lights flashing, telling me that drugs were present. Keeping Megan away from hard drugs was all I ever wanted, and Copper helped me keep her on a straight road.

"Megan stayed away from hard drugs for a while. She started attending rehab and it looks really promising, at least for now.

"I am much more contented and relaxed," Trudy added.

"She now only smokes dope to keep her calm; she has more self-control now, considering the state she's in. But she's not coping well with her morning sickness and smoking some pot makes her feel better. Besides, it's not like she is on hard drugs. Marijuana is not that addictive. Anyway … it should be made legal. I don't understand what that fuss is all about. Alcohol is legal and much more addictive and dangerous than smoking a joint or two.

"That's why I allowed Megan to grow a few pots of marijuana in our backyard. She brought home some good seedlings. Now we have a good crop for our use." Trudy whispered this, worried that somebody may see or overhear this unusual conversation.

"Did you say grow your own?" Donna asked to clarify.

She fought to keep her right eyebrow down but felt it fighting back.

"Well … yes. I need it too! And I'm under pressure. I wanted to keep Megan home. It's not that difficult, you know. Just like growing tomatoes or peas. Water and sunshine, that's all it takes."

Donna, trying to keep an expression of complete understanding, put her tongue in her cheek.

"There is one problem," Trudy said after a prolonged, nervous chuckle.

"What's that?" asked Donna.

"Bloody dog, Copper; he sniffs around the backyard and digs up the growing marijuana plants. He's ruined so many good plants that we've started storing harvested marijuana plants in the shed, but Copper is now scratching on the shed door, trying to get in and is barking like crazy." Trudy laughed.

"Aren't you worried about someone dobbing you into the law?" Donna asked.

"Not really. We don't have close neighbours. We live on a large block and grow our own vegetables and keep a few chooks, too. I like Daisy to eat healthy foods, without preservatives and all that chemical shit you buy in the supermarket. It's not good for you, you know?"

"But, Trudy, aren't you worried that somebody may report you to the police?" Donna asked.

"I'm not worried about the law. Why should I? Megan spent so much money on ice and heroin, spending money on that shit until nothing was left. We now grow our own weed, and it costs us nothing to produce. Megan has her own cannabis, and so far, she has not been tempted to buy some ice or any other hard drugs.

"That's great, isn't it?" Trudy said, looking for some sort of approval. But Donna didn't respond, and Trudy couldn't stop talking.

"I can tell you that my life is now less complicated. I don't have to worry about how to pay the bills or groceries. Daisy gets a few more toys, too." Trudy giggled in delight.

Whether Trudy was looking for reassurance or sympathy, Donna didn't know, but she gave neither. Trudy, sensing Donna's disapproval of drugs, tried to explain her point.

"Donna, I'm telling you, my back pain is killing me, and I get such bad migraines, too. But after smoking a joint or two, I feel better; it's self-medicating, you know. It helps me sleep. Plus, when Daisy is fast asleep, Megan and I sit with a glass of wine and light up a joint together. We are now much closer than we've ever been. We hardly argue now," Trudy said happily, looking to get approval for her argument. Again none came, but Donna was curious.

"Trudy, aren't you worried that your home might be raided by police or drug thugs? Growing Marijuana is illegal. You could get in a lot of trouble." She shook her head, imagining the ramifications.

"No, not really. What can they do to me? To be honest with you, Donna, I wouldn't mind being locked up for a few weeks to get some rest and catch up on some sleep, but I am only worried about my little Daisy. Who will take care of my poor little girl? Megan needs me too. Besides, I am less worried now since Megan brought home a huge new dog – a big Rottweiler – to protect her stash. We call him Rambo. He can smell cops or anybody else coming a mile away. He'd alert us if they were coming. Megan trained him well; nobody would dare enter our home as Rambo will rip them to shreds. The only problem is I have to keep Copper locked inside the house: Rambo would eat him for breakfast."

"Trudy, that means you can't bring Rambo to the small dog enclosure."

"Oh, no, I would never bring Rambo to the Dog Club. He is a vast, barrel-chested, fully-grown vicious dog – a real killing machine. Nobody would mess with our Rambo," Trudy laughed nervously.

Donna stood and thanked Trudy for the cappuccino and cake, excusing herself as she had to get home on time to take Isabella to her hip-hop dancing class. Trudy hugged Donna, thanking her for being a good listener …

As they parted, Donna was relieved that this lunch was finally over. She had no intentions of meeting with Trudy again.

More than a few months went by without Trudy's appearance. Then one day, she came in an unusually jovial mood. Leading excited Copper through the entrance gate, she unleashed him and let him run off to the other dogs and then walked to the bench and plonked down next to Donna. She seemed very satisfied and pleased with herself. Donna couldn't wait any longer.

"So what's been happening lately in your life?" she asked.

"A lot," said Trudy with a grin. "Megan is due any time now. When the baby is born, things will get much easier."

"How's that?" someone asked.

"Megan will register as my carer. And as a single mother with two children, she will receive more than I could ever hope to get a measly old age pension as a grandparent. This way, we will all survive much better. That's the only way we can get back at the government."

Trudy scanned the other ladies' faces and continued. "I don't feel all that guilty. I have diabetes and have terrible back pain … and I struggle to work around the garden. Megan is helpful around the house, so considering that grandparents don't get extra money for what we do, this is the best option available to us.

"We are saving the government millions of dollars in taking care of grandchildren for free. Grandparents are invisible. Nobody cares about us. How come Foster parents get paid and the grandparents get nothing. I'm really pissed off with that deal. It's not fair, is it?"

Beverly nodded in agreement, probably still scared to disagree with Trudy.

More months passed without Trudy attending the Dog Club; nobody had seen her. Then, one day, she turned up pushing a big pram with a peacefully sleeping baby boy; but no dog.

The first thing Amelia asked was, "What's happened to Copper? Where is he?"

Trudy shrugged matter-of-factly. "Cooper developed some sort of dog cancer. He was in a lot of pain, so I had to put him down."

One of Donna's eyebrows rose and she looked at Trudy and thought, *Yeah, you had to get rid of Copper because he was demolishing your weed plants … or maybe Rambo ate him for breakfast.*

She knew Trudy kept many secrets. But she knew that

she had no right to judge her, either. Trudy was only trying to survive the best way she knew how. She was alone and forced to be self-reliant; she was doing something she believed would save her daughter, but it was all delusional because it had no lasting positive outcome, no future. Cannabis would give her a false sense of security. Eventually, Megan would go back to using heroin, like before, and Trudy would end up looking after two grandchildren and one still very sick daughter.

She pushed the thought away. Seeing Trudy so radiant and happy was all that mattered at this moment. She was glowing with pride, showing off her six-week-old grandson.

"His name is Samuel, Sammy for short, after his granddad, my ex-husband," Trudy said with nostalgia. Donna could see the longing in Trudy's eyes for her past life and her husband, who had been her only true love.

"Sammy has the most beautiful blue eyes, just like his granddad," she boasted. "Every time I look at Sammy, he reminds me how much my ex-husband had missed out on, not knowing his two grandkids.

"I'll tell you what, ladies," Trudy said, suddenly looking pleased with herself, "for all the struggles, pain and suffering, Daisy and Sammy have brought genuine joy to my life."

Ever so gently, Trudy lifted her grandson from the pram and passed him around from one person to the next.

When Donna's turn came, she stopped for a moment, looking at a newborn in her arms. Glancing at Sammy's deep blue eyes, she admired the miracle of nature, a newborn baby, another human being made in God's image, and wondered why God abandoned some of these innocent children.

When Trudy's turn came again, after all the cuddles from the rest of the group, she held her little bundle of joy in her arms and said, "I am really blessed and glad to have my daughter and her kids all living with me under the same roof. I wouldn't change my place with anybody in the world. In the end, it is all worth it … don't you think so, ladies?" Trudy smiled.

"Of course, it is," came the instant response from everyone.

As the grandmothers parted, all walking home with their beloved pooches, Donna turned and waved.

"Bye, for now, Trudy, and best of luck with your new baby boy. See you all tomorrow, same place, same time ….

That was the last time Trudy came to the Dog Club. Nobody has seen her since that day. Somebody heard that Trudy had moved to a country town … to escape from some bikers Megan was mixing with. Others speculated Trudy sold her place and moved up north, hiding away to protect her grandchildren …

Nobody really knew what had really happened. However, everybody agreed that Megan and her two kids would be safe because their grandmother, Trudy, would always look after them.

Two Mothers

As Donna prepared dinner on a late summer afternoon, the phone rang.

"Hello, my name is Elvira. I've found your puppy. Did you, by any chance, lose a black puppy, a charcoal poodle?" she asked.

"No. You got the wrong number. Our puppy is snow white. Bon-Bon is sleeping in the backyard under the trampoline."

But Donna had a bad feeling. *What if Bon-Bon got out. She could easily squeeze her tiny body through the fence when Tom was pruning roses.* She panicked and rushed outside. Izzy followed in a panic, too. Bon-Bon was nowhere in sight.

Donna's voice trembled with fear as she started quizzing the person on the other line. "Is she okay? I don't know how she got out. She loves chasing birds. She must have disappeared without me noticing?"

"Don't worry. Your pup is perfectly okay. She got stuck in the mud in the lake and is covered in black. She's a little scared but very dirty. I dragged her out. My grandkids helped me wash her up. I saw your phone number on her collar, so I called you."

Donna could not listen. She just wanted to get Elvira's address and drive … fly … and run as fast she could to get her beloved Bon-Bon, thinking, *Oh my God, Izzy would be devastated if she lost Bon-Bon.*

Donna's drive to pick up Bon-Bon was only a short distance from her home. Elvira and her husband, Yohan, lived only a few streets away.

Donna's heart pounded as if it would jump out of her chest. Little Izzy was unusually quiet, but as soon as they rang the doorbell and she heard Bon-Bon barking, she jumped up and down with excitement.

The moment Elvira opened the door, Izzy ran inside, frantically calling Bon-Bon's name, overjoyed to be reunited with her puppy. They kissed, hugged and licked like they'd been apart for a lifetime.

The first thing Elvira said was, "I know how you must feel. I used to have a black poodle. Her name was Lulu, and she was part of our family. When she died, I cried for days. I swore I would never get another puppy."

Donna detected the strong German accent coming from this chubby woman with the oval face, high cheekbones and broad, friendly smile. She felt instantly at ease.

Donna introduced herself as Elvira brought in her two little grandkids. The kids didn't hang around long as they were busy chasing Bon-Bon all around the backyard.

"I've got grandkids this weekend," Elvira said. "I took them to the lake to feed the ducks. As kids were throwing bread, seagulls started pinching the best bits, so the kids got bored and went for a run around the lake.

"Then we noticed your puppy. She appeared out of nowhere, jumped in, and swam possessed, trying to reach ducks. They were rather agitated as their nests are hidden among the water lilies. I realised your pup was getting tired and started calling her to come out. When she heard my voice, she swam towards me in the shallow, muddy area.

"That's when she got bogged in that sticky mud. She was stuck and all muddied up in black sludge. I rolled up my pants, got into the mud, and got her before she got too distressed.

"My goodness, she was *black*. We ran home and started hosing her down and got soaking wet as the grandkids tried to catch her." Elvira giggled. "What fun that was!

"As soon as we all were washed and dried, I called you." She looked pleasantly at Donna. "Why don't I make you a cuppa? If you have time, that is. My husband went fishing, and he won't be home for hours. Besides, look at our grandchildren: they are having so much fun chasing your Bon-Bon all around the yard."

"That would be lovely. And thanks for saving Bon-Bon. That was the best phone call I got in my entire life." She was so grateful and more than happy to oblige. Besides, Izzy was so happy playing with her new friends, so she need not hurry home.

As they started chatting, they realised they had a lot in common. Both women were migrants with similar moral values and cultural habits; caring for the grandchildren created another bond and mutual respect.

"I do bookkeeping from home while Yohan is busy building boats at the Fremantle shipyard," Elvira told Donna. "We have so many orders and insufficient qualified staff, so poor Yohan works day and night. There are not enough hours in a day. When I had a dog, I took the time to go for walks, now I spend all my free time with my grandkids. I get so exhausted sometimes."

The afternoon stretched to evening as they chatted away – so many stories to tell but not enough time. Then Donna realised, "Tom will be worried about how far we probably had to drive to bring home Bon-Bon. We had better be going."

They were practically neighbours, and from that day every afternoon when Donna took Bon-Bon for a walk, she would stop and chat with Elvira. Her grandkids were around Izzy's age, and on weekends the two grandmothers started taking the kids to the playground or to other kids' activities.

One day, while having lunch together at the foreshore, Elvira looked at Donna and smiled.

"Donna, it must have been destiny for us to meet. When I lost my Lulu, I was devastated. She must have guided me to the lake to save your Bon-Bon. A life full of so many delightful coincidences," Elvira said softly while getting emotional.

"Oh, no, my dear new friend, nothing is a coincidence. I think that our lives have been pre-destined. I always knew that my granddaughter would come into our lives. She found us. Isabella was a gift from God, an angel that saved so many lives." Donna fell silent, and put her hands to her mouth to stop the unspoken words. But she knew deep down in her heart that Izzy had saved her father from sinking into a deep black hole of despair. Izzy had given him a new purpose and a will to live. *God knows, but possibly one day Izzy may save her mother too.*

Donna didn't want to think or imagine her life before or after Izzy. She had always been here with her. However, she didn't feel it was right to share such an emotional and spiritual story with anybody, or burden Elvira with her problems.

Their friendship became mutual and developed even further when Yohan invited Tom and Donna to fish off the Fremantle coast. Sinking a few crayfish pots was such a novelty, and they ended up with fresh seafood for the weekend barbecue.

During the summer, they took the grandkids to Rottnest Island, Penguin and Seal Island. Frequently, both families picnicked under the shade of pencil pines and eucalyptus trees at the Rockingham foreshore where the children splashed on the beach and built sandcastles together.

Tom and Donna often visited Elvira and Yohan at their holiday home in Mandurah where the kids loved playing in the estuary's shallow waters. Looking for crabs was always an adventure for them … and grown-ups too.

The luxury boat docked in the estuary canals, right in front of the house. They were a wealthy couple, but humble enough not to show off or make Tom and Donna feel in any way inferior to them. They had no financial problems and planned their perfect retirement of sailing around the world in their new boat that Yohan was so proudly building, all by himself., Their plans, however, were permanently derailed when their son Michael and his wife divorced. Sarah, like most biological mothers, became a single mum to their two children.

Michael worked in a remote area as a Fly-In-Fly-Out worker – a FIFO – working two weeks on and two weeks off. He spent time with his kids when he came home. Because he worked offshore on an oil rig, when he came home, he stayed with his parents.

Michael tried to rebuild his life, but finances became a

complicated affair. In the divorce settlement, the sale of the family home benefitted Sarah the most, and she was awarded half his superannuation and half of his shares. Sarah even claimed his frequent flyer points, too. She received whatever she asked for. She was, however, unreliable, often partying with her new friends, and was on the lookout for a new relationship. Elvira and Yohan stepped in, providing support and care for their grandchildren until the parents could resolve their marital issues.

When Sarah started neglecting the kids, they had no option but to report the neglect to the child protection authorities. Elvira and Yohan wanted support from DCP in finding an amicable solution with their daughter-in-law to keep her two young children safe as Sarah had become depressed and self-medicated with alcohol and drugs.

One day, when Donna and Elvira met for a cappuccino at the foreshore, Elvira was beside herself with worry.

"So what happened with DCP?" Donna wanted to know.

"We have had a few meetings already. At the mediation, we agreed to temporarily take care of our grandkids while Sarah goes into rehabilitation to deal with her addiction and gets counselling to manage her depression and anxiety."

"That's great news!" Donna gushed. "So Sarah finally agreed to go to rehab."

"Yes, we are happy too. Sarah can visit us any time she wants to see her kids, but she hardly ever comes. The kids miss her. I tried to phone her a few times, but she always found some excuses."

"Oh, I am so sorry to hear that. I know how you feel. Isabella's mum has not turned up to see her baby since

Izzy's first birthday."

"Let's hope this will improve soon. Sarah loves her kids. I am sure she will change."

After that day, Donna didn't hear from Elvira for a while, so she called her.

"What is up, Elvira? I wanted to know how you are doing. Are there any fresh developments with DCP?"

"Oh yeah, we got some good news." Elvira had a bounce in her voice that Donna had not heard for quite a while. "Sarah kept her word. This time she has stayed with rehab, and counselling sessions helped with her mental health issues, too. The DCP approved, and the kids are happy to live with their mum. We give her support if she asks for it.

"The good news is that Michael and Sarah have patched up their differences now, and he spends more time with kids – of course, as his work schedule permits. Those arrangements were made between themselves, so the kids are much happier now."

"Oh, that is terrific news. I am so pleased for you and Yohan. You two will now have more time to spend on yourselves." Donna was indeed elated when she heard all that good news.

Months passed before the two friends again had some free time to catch up. Donna knew that Elvira and Yohan were busy renovating their home, so she didn't want to intrude.

One day, after Donna had driven Izzy to pre-school, Elvira called, sobbing on the phone.

"What is wrong?" But Elvira was too distraught to talk.

"Okay. I am coming over," Donna said. "Put on the kettle. I will be at your place soon." She knew something was really wrong as Elvira was one who never complained much. She was always such an optimistic and positive person.

As soon as she arrived, she hugged her friend. "Come on, stop crying and dry your eyes." She led her into the kitchen. "Wow, your new kitchen looks great. What else are you planning to renovate? I can smell vanilla and cinnamon and the apple strudel smells so yummy."

Elvira was well known for her homemade cooking, especially cakes. As she poured cups of percolated coffee, she hurriedly sat down next to Donna and started to tell her story.

"Well, most of the renovation is nearly completed. Next week, new carpets and that is it. I got more problems than worrying about the renovation though."

Donna listened.

"Shortly after I spoke to you last time, Sarah applied for a job at one of Perth's biggest accountancy firms, and she got the job on the spot. She told me she was excited about her new job and her financial independence. I told her I was so happy for her.

"Then, one day, when she came over to pick up her kids, she told me something that shocked me at first, but I kind of suspected that something was odd."

Elvira stopped for a moment and licked her spoon full of fresh cream. She looked up at Donna and hesitated.

"Yeah, what? Do not stop. You cannot keep me in suspense." Donna's eyebrow rose, prompting her friend to continue.

"Sarah told me that after her counselling sessions, she gained new confidence. She told me she needed to explore her hidden desires."

"What was that? That is something new." Donna's lips twisted, and her eyes grew wider. *What was coming now?* "What desire is Sarah talking about?"

"Well … she's experimenting with her desire to explore her bio-sexuality further."

"Huh? What brought that up?" She looked more shocked.

"That must have been one of the reasons Sarah left Michael. He never told us much about his relationship with Sarah; therefore, this totally shocked me." Elvira stared at the table and shook her head. "She told me she is in love and moving in with her new girlfriend."

"Gee, that is fast," Donna commented and rolled her eyes.

"When … how did Sarah meet her new love."

The two friends sipped their coffee and Elvira served up a second slice of apple strudel. "Let me tell you the story from the beginning," Elvira said.

"Sarah met her new lover at work. Samantha was her immediate supervisor."

"Did you say … Samantha?"

"Yes, you heard me right. Samantha is a woman much older than Sarah, with more work experience, power, and influence.

"Sarah told me that Sam, which is what she calls her, is divorced with two pre-school kids. They soon became friends. Best friends … with benefits. Samantha lured young Sarah into her love web."

"According to Sarah, it was love at first sight and what she had secretly craved all of her adult life but was scared to explore. Sarah was so happy, telling me she had found her true love and that Sam had swept her off her feet.

"The lovebirds and their four kids soon moved in together. Samantha has a vast new home and a substantial amount of money from her alimony settlement from her ex-husband, the father of her two children.

"As money was not a problem, Sarah quit work to stay at home and be mum while Sam continued working. Sarah was now solely dependent on Sam's income and generosity.

"They did not hide their lesbian relationship. All their friends thought that living with two mums was perfectly normal too. However, one big problem they kept hidden was that they liked to smoke pot, which led to harder drugs. Sam had started using heroin after she split with her husband and admitted it. She went to rehab a few times but never stayed off it for more than a few months. Since her divorce, she now had more money to splurge on drugs.

"Sarah tried to convince me she was a casual user – as she unblushingly claimed." Elvira shook her head again.

"The two mums entertained often, and the four kids were left unsupervised. My youngest granddaughter has asthma. Sometimes I have to take the poor child to a doctor; sometimes she is so bad that I have had to rush her to the hospital.

"Well, the two mothers promised me that everything was good in their household, telling me not to worry as the kids were being well looked after. Sam's kids were spending most of their time with their grandparents, too. Sam objected little as long as her ex-husband was paying alimony on time. She never complained. She liked her freedom."

"Yohan and I were not deceived though, so I reported two mothers to DCP for neglecting their four kids while both of them were getting high. We demanded that child protection authorities intervene to ensure that the mothers stop using drugs and alcohol and provided a safe home for these poor children.

"So, what happened?" Donna wanted to know.

"After the first meeting with DCP," Elvira went on, "we suggested the kids stay with their respective grandparents to provide a safe home environment. DCP suggested that both mothers should attend rehabilitation.

"That arrangement was to be in place only for a few months. After the treatment, the two mothers were to be randomly tested to ensure long-term sobriety."

"That's great. DCP is doing what they are supposed to do!" Donna stated happily.

"Hang on, Donna. Not that fast." Elvira held her hand up to stop her friend's quick conclusion.

"Yeah, sure enough, the child protection authorities took immediate action. I was so impressed with their effort until I found out …"

"Found out what?" Donna's interest was now seriously spiked.

"Well, DCP called Sarah and Sam on their house phone and informed them about us complaining and demanding that they be randomly tested. After an hour of discussion on a phone speaker, DCP insisted that at least one mother promised not to be stoned or intoxicated while caring for their children.

"Of course, the two mothers wholeheartedly agreed to

comply with the DCP request. That was that. What the two love birds did behind their doors was nobody's business."

"Oh, Donna, Yohan is mad as hell, but we are powerless. We don't want to upset Sarah; otherwise, she won't bring the kids to our place."

"Oh, Elvira, I am so sorry. Unfortunately, the biological mothers are always in charge. That's more or less always the same story. I hear the same story from so many other grandparents too."

"It's madness. How can DCP believe that somebody who is using drugs will stop? Sarah promised so many times but never stuck with it? I am so upset, I can tell you. And Yohan was so furious with DCP. He wanted to go there and kick the door down. I stopped him, of course. Otherwise, he would have ended up locked up instead of them.

"A few days later, when we calmed down, we went back to the DCP. However, that is not all. When we went back to DCP to complain, nobody listened to us.

"As far as the child protection authorities were concerned, problem solved. The first part of two lesbian mothers has been resolved, bluntly telling us to back off and give mothers some breathing space.

"DCP got sick of us coming to the office, and on our last meeting with DCP, they reprimanded us, telling us that two mothers were doing well.

"When kids go to sleep, the mothers may smoke or have a few drinks. We got labelled as being old-fashioned, stereotyped by our cultural beliefs that two women shouldn't love each other.

"One of the case managers was very abrupt, telling us bluntly, 'Just because the two mothers are lesbians, they shouldn't be discriminated against it. That is something that the older generation has difficulty accepting'. They told us that times have changed and we need to adjust to new social norms. They said 'the two mothers have a right to bring up their kids without being harassed or falsely accused'. DCP believes that, in their opinion, both mothers were wonderful parents!"

Elvira put her head down, her face with anger.

"That made us even more furious. The child protection authorities sidetracked the drug issue by accusing us of cultural bias against the lesbian relationship. "It's not bloody right, is it, Donna? Just because we are migrants from Germany – European conservatives – we should be told what to do or how to adjust our behaviours." Elvira's eyes moistened with tears. "We only want to protect our grandkids. What's wrong with that?"

Donna squeezed Elvira's hands as she gently reassured her friend. "Sadly, DCP seemed more concerned with adults' wellbeing, primarily biological mothers, more than anything else."

Donna nodded. "Drug abuse is conveniently seen as an illness … with the political ideology. So who will argue against it? Only the grandparents, and we carry little weight these days."

But Elvira didn't give up. She went back to the child protection authorities and complained again. And again, their accusations fell on deaf ears. Every time Elvira went to their office to complain, she would deal with a new staff member who didn't know or didn't care about their case. Staff turnover and almost certainly a lack of proper training only made matters worse. They would say to Elvira:

"Stop being judgmental, and offer these lesbian couples some emotional support, understanding, and empathy." Still, the child protection authorities promised to investigate the allegations of children's neglect.

Of course, Elvira demanded to know the outcome of such an investigation but could not get any information due to privacy laws. When she confronted her daughter-in-law and demanded to know what the child protection authorities had done to ensure the children's safety, she was told to mind her own business.

Concerned for her two grandkids' well-being and the other two kids living there as well, Elvira was determined not to give up. But every time Elvira arrived at the house to check on the children, Sarah would scream at the top of her voice.

"If you ever come to my front door again, I will take out a restraining order against you. If you care about your grandchildren, make your son Michael pay up what he owes on his child support and be less concerned about my lifestyle! Just because, now and then, I use drugs, that doesn't make me a terrible mother. I am sick and tired of your interference, criticism and judgments!"

After a while, Elvira and Yohan stopped complaining. It was pointless. Nobody took them seriously. Nobody cared.

They made a conscious decision. Step back, give two mothers more space, become more tolerant, but continue supporting their grandchildren. Elvira and Yohan realised that this was the best deal they would ever get. Their focus shifted from "two mothers" to their two grandchildren.

They started taking kids to sporting activities, school assemblies, organised birthday parties, Christmas shows and other children's activities. All that cost extra money. No cash was offered from either of the mothers. Elvira and Yohan stopped complaining out of fear that the mothers would not allow them to see their grandkids. The only thing that mattered was to keep kids safe.

The two mothers had all the parental rights and all the authority that went with it. Elvira and Yohan had no power and were too scared to rock that boat. The two mothers were legally in charge of their children, and the grandparents accepted that fact.

They were all in the same wobbly boat, one that could sink quickly. Elvira and Yohan decided it was best to plug the holes in that fragile boat and keep the kids happy and safe. Staying quiet and not upsetting the two mothers was their only option. Maintaining harmony and providing a happy childhood for their grandchildren became their only aim.

Eventually, the two mothers learned grandparents could be perfect babysitters, too, so they backed off and used their services freely. Their relationship improved. Of course, the beneficiaries were the children.

One day, while lunching together, Donna praised her friends for being so diplomatic and wise. "Your grandchildren are lucky to have you in their lives. I only wonder about other children who don't have such support. Who cares about them? Who takes them to outdoor entertainment, and attends the school assemblies and sports carnivals, and other enchanted adventures and the magical world of Christmas?"

Elvira sighed deeply. "Grandparents are the safety net that all children who are in trouble turn to. Without us, there would be so many more damaged and lost kids. That is what grandparents do: we look after our grandkids, no matter what …" She nodded optimistically. "That is what grandparents do …"

Thankfully, such kind and wise people exist on this earth. They are grandparents.

The Crafty Lot

Donna had met her friend, Penny, while she was working and needed a house cleaner. Penny had owned a cleaning company and had come highly recommended, and the two had become firm friends. When Donna retired, Penny had encouraged her to join the local Arts and Craft group.

The Arts and Craft group was a multi-cultural, diverse bunch of grandmothers. Some women from the K-9 group had joined the Arts and Crafters too, and most had one thing in common: they provided care for their grandchildren. Some women had a talent for painting with oils, some with watercolours. A few made pottery and sculptures while some liked to draw. Then there were those who were keen on embroidery, quilting, knitting and crocheting, and some got pleasure from making paper flowers.

When Donna took on the role of carer for Isabella, Izzy became her first and only obligation. She had no option but to take early retirement. She let go of her career with a heavy heart, not from the financial loss, as significant as it was, but from losing the daily contact and interaction with people. Donna craved this the most. She had always enjoyed being actively involved in the community. It gave her a sense of purpose and personal pride. Hence, joining the Arts and Craft group was an excellent opportunity for socialising and having fun.

The Arts and Craft group struggled financially, and their bank account was chronically in the red. To remedy the situation, Donna suggested Penny leave the Art Gallery and instead meet at members' houses, rotating turns. Each member could supply morning tea at his or her home on the monthly rotational roster. And so a smaller, more adventurous group of grannies formed. A gold coin was collected as a monthly donation from each member to improve the coffers.

The first independent meeting took place at Donna's and on that morning, after the general meeting, and a few cups of coffee and cakes, Donna asked, "Who wants to be the treasurer?"

Penny was the only one who volunteered. She was therefore elected unanimously, with universal applause.

Penny was thereafter appropriately nicknamed 'Money Penny'. She became club secretary and treasurer and assigned with fundraising and money collecting during their monthly get-togethers. She also came up with a new name for the group, 'The Crafty Lot'. Nobody objected.

The group had regular fundraising events – garage sales, cupcake sales and so on – and sold arts and crafts in the market to build up the group's savings and to pay for their occasional luncheons. However, this time, Penny, the event organiser, couldn't decide on an activity and asked for suggestions.

"Melbourne Cup lunch," a few shouted in unison.

And so, The Crafty Lot went to a Melbourne Cup luncheon. It was the perfect time to relax and focus on having fun rather than dwelling on the problems at home. Some of the Crafty Lot grannies enjoyed gambling and would often hop on a shuttle bus from the Senior Centre to the Perth Crown Casino to try their luck on the poker machine. The fortunate ones generously shared their winnings, buying food and drinks for others in the group who weren't so lucky that day.

Penny was a slender woman with a big heart, and Donna couldn't but admire her courage and determination when she faced the tragic events of her life. It all started when her daughter Kylie was diagnosed with breast cancer. Her husband couldn't cope with her illness and shot through, leaving Kylie and her infant daughter Rachel behind.

Penny was there all the way throughout Kyle's darkest days of chemotherapy. Kylie fought bravely but sadly lost her battle with cancer when Rachel started primary school. Penny had no time to grieve for losing her daughter. She just moved on with her life. Her job was now to raise her granddaughter. Overnight, Penny became Rachel's mother and her grandmother, too.

Penny was a well-educated woman with a university degree. In her younger days, she worked as a bookkeeper for a prominent accountant firm. She formed a private cleaning business as this gave her time and flexibility that her accountancy office job didn't. Rachael was an outstanding basketball player, and Penny took her all over the state for her training and competitions.

When her cleaning business expanded, Penny secured a significant contract with a prominent accounting firm in a city high-rise building. That job Penny kept strictly for herself, telling Donna: "Knowing an excellent accountant may come in handy one day."

By then, Rachel was in her last year at UWA, studying

commercial accounting and tax laws. Donna was not surprised when Penny told her that Rachael got her internship at the famous accountant firm where she worked as a cleaner. Penny was very resourceful.

Ian, Penny's husband, worked as a carpenter but had an accident at work and lost four fingers. For a long while, Ian couldn't work. During that time, Penny was the sole breadwinner. However, Money-Penny was resourceful with the bit of money she had and learned to survive on a shoestring budget. She lived up to the challenge splendidly, without complaint or any sign of grief. Like most incredible grannies in the world – if stoicism is considered a virtue – facing daily challenges and adversity, Penny's stoic endurance was not based on her emotionless surrender to a cruel fate, but on her courage and self-control in recognising what she could change and what she could not, without losing hope of better times ahead.

In one of their meetings, Penny asked, "Ladies, come on, you Crafty Lot, put your heads together. Where would you like to go for the Melbourne Cup luncheon? We need to find a venue. Who's got some suggestions?

A few ideas were offered, but all were dismissed. Then Penny turned to Donna.

"Donna, you know a few people in the tourism and hospitality industry. Perhaps you could get us a good deal with someone you know."

Donna's faint smile, more out of slight discomfort than modesty, promised a solution. "I've lost many contacts in the Hospitality Industry since my retirement, but my friend Evelyn told me that her son owns a pub in South Fremantle. I haven't heard from her for a while, but I'll chase her up and will let you know."

In the past, she and Evelyn had socialised regularly, but their life circumstances had forced them in different directions. For Donna and her husband Tom, their priority had shifted to raising Isabella. That was their new alternative lifestyle. There was no more time to socialise with their friends. No, more dancing, swinging around the floor with Tom. The only swinging left in Donna's life was pushing Izzy on the swings in the local playgrounds.

No more cocktail parties, dining at the finest restaurants. Instead, Donna's culinary experience strengthened. She became an expert in making cupcakes with rainbow colours, bread with hundreds and thousands, sausage rolls and chicken nuggets. They both enjoyed concerts at WASO (West Australian Symphony Orchestra); now all that was replaced with Izzy's sing-alongs. They would often perform a musical duet, like, *if you're happy and you know it, clap your hands* … Indeed, Donnas' life spun around like in the kids' song: the wheels on the bus go round and round, all day long …

True to her word, Donna made a few calls and tracked down her old work colleague, Evelyn, who now lived in Broome, WA. To everyone's delight, a booking was confirmed at *The Old Pub,* which Evelyn's son Ian owned and had restored to its magnificent colonial glory. The booking, secured with a special discounted offer, included a buffet lunch with a glass of wine or cocktail. Evelyn was excited that her work colleague Tanya would be attending, and promised to take a flight down to Perth in time to join the group for the Melbourne Cup celebrations.

A week before the Melbourne Cup, the Crafty Lot busily

created fancy hats for the event, delighted that Elizabeth had offered to design some unique hats for the event. Donna called her Twiggy for her slim, tall stature. Elizabeth had actually modelled for Harrods store in London in her youthful days. Even now, past her seventies, she still walked like a model. A few days before the cup, the entire group met again at Elizabeth's house for the final rehearsal dress up. Penny and Elizabeth inspected all the hats, and added some final touches here and there. Everyone unpacked the dresses they would wear for that special occasion as they were shown around for the inspection. It raised a few giggles, some laughter, and jokes about several gypsy style dresses.

The Crafty Lot is going to be the best dressed there, Donna thought. *We'll be the centre of attention.*

Elizabeth had promised the group that everybody would wear something special, colourful, and outrageous, and she delivered. The Crafty Lot looked stunning.

Melbourne Cup Day arrived, and Donna went there early to meet her dear friend Evelyn. Due to Covid-19, she had requested a table in the garden, out in the open air. "Besides, some of the Crafty Lot may get over-excited and rowdy," she explained with a smile. "This is perfect setting for a party – beautiful old pub, on a heritage list – in South Fremantle."

Indeed, its garden was stunning, full of lovely greenery, with flourishing flowerbeds and shrubs, where small birds chirped happily and hopped about within the tangled undergrowth. The Old Pub's historical integrity and aesthetic appeal were the principal attraction of post-colonial times, and a perfect ambience where the elderly ladies could celebrate Melbourne Cup.

When the Crafty Lot arrived, the Pub was a hive of activity and joy. Ladies picked a horse with an unusual or funny name, placed a few dollars on a race sweepstake, and with tickets in hand, they were ready for one of the most famous horse races in the world. On this first Tuesday in November, the entire country stopped to watch the Melbourne Cup. Even though not yet declared an official public holiday, everybody went out for lunch on that day, whether at home or at work. The race celebration was kept low key because of Covid-19 restrictions. But the race was celebrated regardless. It didn't dampen the grandmothers' enthusiasm to have fun, and almost everyone placed a small bet.

Meanwhile, at the Pub, the Flemington Racecourse's main event was still a few hours away, the Crafty Lot gathered around Jennifer, who was first at the bar. Jennifer had dressed in black body-hugging leather hot pants and a silver glitter tee shirt. She had tied her wavy black hair up with a gigantic silver bow. Jenny knew exactly what she wanted to order from the bar, and advised each of the others what to choose, describing each cocktail in detail. She seemed quite an expert.

"Jennifer, where have you learned so much about the aperitifs and cocktails?" Donna asked.

"I was once a barmaid," she replied with a most charming smile. "I've worked in pubs for most of my life but had to quit my job when I was stuck raising two grandkids that my daughter left behind. Who knows where she is … probably getting drunk with her new boyfriend in some godforsaken pub. I haven't heard from her in ages, and I hope I don't see her too soon. She is nothing but trouble." Jenny's expression, however, betrayed her deep concern.

"The girls are nearly teenagers now and almost old enough to take care of themselves, so I will have more time for myself. I work part-time as a cleaner in the local pub. I go to work very early in the morning when the girls are still asleep, and I get home before they go to school. I'd like to go back to work in the bar, but who would want to employ me now. I am too old for that job."

"But, Jenny, with your experience, you can still work in a pub," Valerie encouraged.

"Don't be silly. Only young chicks with firm boobs and sexy bums can get a job in the pub. Look at me! No man would want to buy a beer from me!"

"Look at you, Jenny. You look so sexy," someone else made a comment.

"Oh yeah? Who do you think you are kidding?" Jenny laughed. "I will soon turn sixty. I'm an old chook now."

Valerie laughed. "You are only sixty! Wait until you get to my age. Besides, old chooks, the old boilers make a wonderful soup."

"What is that we hear, Jenny, that you got a new man in your life?" Penny asked.

"Yeah. I met Trevor online. He has awakened an old dragon in me, spitting fire with the passion that must have been buried deep inside. Trevor moved in with me and my girls, and they approve of him too. That's important to me. When we are together, life is never boring. I go to work, and he goes to the golf course. He is crazy about golf. I can't understand what he sees in that tedious game. Chasing that little white ball all over the field is not my cup of tea.

"When I get home from work, the girls go to school, and the house is all ours. It's a good feeling to have a man in my life. I've been single for so many years, being a mother and grandmother to my girls, I forgot what it feels like to be a woman.

"That is such good news. Enjoy this time in your life. When you get to my age, it is all but over," Anne replied.

In her mid-sixties, Beverly, or Bev as they called her, looked radiant in a well-fitted ruby-red dress and a pink azalea flower band in her hair.

"Bev, you've cut your hair short. And that burgundy really suits you. It looks really good. Good on you. On another score, has your granddaughter moved out?" Anne delved.

"She sure has. Alison and her fiancé moved out six months ago. They brought their first home together. And she's now a qualified dental nurse." Bev smiled, showing off her new dentures. "Ladies, if you want your teeth polished and cleaned, I'll ask my Alison, so you get some discount too.

"Funny though … when she moved out, I felt so alone. I really, really missed her. And the house was so empty. I was so bored that I took up ballroom dancing just to get out of the house."

"Hooray! Bev, it's about bloody time you did something for yourself," someone yelled from the back.

Jenny returned from the bar, carrying a tall glass full of rainbow colours, layers of fruit juices decorated with lime, watermelon, and two tiny umbrellas.

"Thanks, Jenny," Bev said, then looked apprehensively at all the colours.

"Don't worry, Bev. It's a mocktail – no alcohol. You are safe with us," Jenny reassured her with a tender smile.

The Crafty Lot knew of Bev's tragic past and supported Bev's sobriety. Bev had escaped from a violent husband and had struggled on her own as a single mum for years. But when her only son Matt died in a horrific motorbike accident, Bev's life fell apart. To numb her pain and sorrow, she turned to alcohol. Matt's girlfriend was so young, that she couldn't cope with raising a newborn baby. With DCP support, the agreement was reached and a parenting plan was put in place that her granddaughter Alison came to live with Bev. From that day forward, she attended AA. She'd been sober ever since.

Jenny lifted her second glass of wine, and couldn't help stirring the pot. "Come on, Bev, don't be shy. Tell us." Jenny teased her. "Ladies, Bev is in love. She found a fellow."

Bev lowered her head, hiding her smile. Her blush almost matched her dress. Then she said, "Yeah … I met Peter at the Senior Citizens' dance. He's a widower. We get on so well, and he treats me like a lady. I've waited for so long to find someone like Peter."

"Come on, Bev," Jenny pushed. "Tell us some juicy stuff. Finish the story. Did you do it?"

"Oh, stop being so nosy. Leave the poor women alone," Penny defended to spare Bev from further embarrassment.

"No, it's okay. I don't mind telling you girls." Bev lifted her head, blushing even more. "Oh, yeah, sure, we kissed, but we didn't go further." She waved everyone's suspicions away with her hand. "I was too scared, so nervous, but the sparks were still there. It's been so long I forgot what intimacy felt like."

Jenny plopped down in her seat. "Listen, you silly girl, it's just like riding a bicycle. You never really forget. Just try it."

The Crafty Lot burst into laughter.

The group was still waiting for Rhonda to arrive. Penny had organised a taxi for her as she was recovering from a knee operation. When she walked in on crutches, Jenny again headed to the bar to bring her a cocktail. Then Penny announced that they were now all present, and buffet lunch could begin …

When Rhonda got seated as comfortably as she could, Olivia asked, "How have things been with you?"

"Not bad, considering," came the reply. "My grandkids are healthy and doing well at school. They are now staying with their maternal grandmother. We support one another at times like this. It will give me a bit of a break to sort out some of my health issues. Besides, it's good that the kids get the chance to know their other nana too."

"How are you coping with your husband?" Penny asked.

"Not bad now," Rhonda replied, but the group noticed she looked drained. "He is slowly recovering from his stroke. But his dementia is getting worse.

"The other day we went shopping, and he walked away and got lost. I couldn't find him anywhere. Eventually, I tracked him down in a Miller's shop, looking at ladies' clothes. He didn't know where he was or what he was doing there. Next time, I'll put a dog leash on him so he can't get lost again. Luckily, I am now getting support from Silver Chain, so it's easier to manage."

"Good on you, Rhonda. It's about time you take care of yourself," Jenny shouted down the table.

Donna nodded, noting as she lifted her glass of wine. *That seems to be our catch-cry – take care of yourself.*

"Okay, you Crafty Lot," Penny's voice came from the end of the table, "now that we are all together, let us get stuck into the food."

The buffet table was enormous, full of fresh delights: many meat dishes, varieties of salads and an overflowing mountain of red lava – beautiful fresh prawns. The motto of a buffet lunch is 'Eat as much as you can', so why not! Most of the grannies in the group, because of a tight financial budget, hadn't tasted prawns since last year's Christmas, and seeing so many prawns on offer were suddenly in a frenzy.

Like feeding piranhas in the Amazon River, Donna grinned inwardly as they stacked their plates with as many yummy prawns as they could fit. Some prawns inevitably rolled down the tall stacks and fell to the floor but were quickly dispatched under the table with their foot so no one would notice.

Further away, the fashion parade was about to start so the Crafty Lot returned to the buffet table for more prawns. This time, to Donna's great embarrassment, a lot of prawns were feverishly shoved into the grannies' big handbags. Again, a few ended up on the floor because of the ladies' haste.

The buzz of excitement filled the air as the glamour of the fashion parade maintained prime focus. Elizabeth stood at centre stage, elegantly dressed in a cream silk suit, linen-laced hat ornamented with gardenia flowers. She paraded along the catwalk, turning like the model she used to be to display her outfit, encouraging the other ladies to do the same. Most of them did. The audience appreciated the elderly ladies' courage and rewarded them with enthusiastic applause.

But not everything went according to Penny's plan. When Rhonda bent down to rub her swollen legs, her pants split in half right down the middle.

Spontaneous bursts of laughter smothered her shriek.

"Ooh no …" Penny said, horrified. "Get one of the biggest hats to cover Rhonda behind."

More laughter erupted as Penny produced her broad feathered hat. Evelyn ran to the kitchen and returned with a big apron, which she quickly wrapped around Rhonda's rotund waistline.

Then the main race was about to start, and the atmosphere in the room built to a crescendo. At last, the prawns were forgotten. The race began as the horses leapt out of the starting gates. Screams and cries of support filled the air. Many stood up at the table and ecstatically cheered their mounts on with their arms. The noise swelled. There were more screams. Finally, it reached the climax, and a wild and deafening roar burst out as the horses crossed the line, followed by a brief subsiding clamour of winners' triumphant howls and losers' moans of disappointment.

While waiting for desserts and coffee, some women unzipped their restrictive clothing to breathe a little easier. They could now relax, and the Crafty Lot started chatting again.

Valerie, another joker in the group, looked a million bucks in a colourful silk dress, high heels shoes and decorative wild-berry purple paper hat. She stood up and took a seductive pose.

"Ladies …" She started turning around for all to see. "What do you think of my fancy-looking dress? I spend hours looking around at all the Salvos shops. So do you approve? Look at me!

"I want to keep myself young-looking and trendy. I even got a new tattoo on my ankle. Why not! Isn't it super-cool?"

"You look gorgeous, Valerie," came from all around the table.

"And what do you think of my sexy hairdo, girls? This short style will keep me away from the expensive hairdressers for quite a while and save me money. Isn't it good?"

"But why purple?" Donna asked.

"To match my outfit, of course. I want my grandson Justin to think of me as one cool Granny," Valerie responded with a cheeky smile.

"You look stunning, Valerie," everybody agreed.

Only Anne sat quietly, but soon she could help herself… "Yeah, Valerie, but nothing we can do will make us look young again. It's the young mums who are having fun, and we are raising their spoiled brats …"

Then Lynne started: "I tell you what, some young parents that I meet are wonderful parents. Most of them are much better parents than we used to be, more connected with their kids. Fathers are helpful in the kitchen, too, doing dishes and washing up. They do much more with kids' sports and are involved with their kids in daily activities. In our time, kids were 'seen, but not heard', sent to bed while adults gathered around barbecues and got pissed."

"Yeah, right." Anne was now annoyed. "If that's the case, then why are today's kids so spoiled and have no respect for anybody?"

"I blame technology," Penny said. "All these gadgets and games; it is going far too fast. Kids have no time to be kids. They learn all that junk on YouTube. Children grow up too fast and have no time to be kids."

"Yeah," Jenny shouted. "That bloody technology will ruin our kids. Look what is going on at schools. Facebook, online bullying. I am worried about my girls. Bullying is everywhere. One girl at their school tried to commit suicide because somebody put a photo on her Facebook. The poor girl was so embarrassed with a false story that she was mucking around in a boys' toilet."

"That's disgusting," Rhonda declared, shaking her head.

"Yes. It's no wonder that kids are so confused, playing games on that machine, staring at the blue screen instead of going out and playing with kids the way we used to.

"These days, everything is instant; games are designed to hook kids, so big businesses can sell them new toys. I feel sorry for these young parents. No wonder they have to work two jobs to buy all these gadgets. The kids need to be entertained, but they should play outside. The fresh air is much better for them than being cooped up behind all these electronics."

As the club treasurer, Penny stood up; it was the only way to bring the group of elderly women to attention. She raised her glass. "Good on you, ladies, for taking your grandkids to camp. They should be connected much more with the environment we live in. It is no wonder kids get bored so quickly these days, spending all that time on iPads and smartphones. It's not much fun, is it?"

Donna then jumped up. "Yes, and it's about time we all

start taking part and spending more time outdoors with our grandkids. Younger parents do spend time with their kids – they go out camping together and doing sports. When I take Izzy to sports, I see how dedicated parents are. And the younger generation is definitely much more aware of protecting our environment than we used to. Kids are now taught to recycle goods, and to look after the oceans and marine species caught in plastic. Sadly, the older generations knew little about environmental problems, but thankfully younger generation is now more aware of them. It should have started much sooner, but I suppose it is never too late to protect our beautiful blue planet. Younger people care more for the environment, that's for sure."

Everyone raised their glasses to that.

As the Crafty Lot was finishing their meals, Evelyn turned to Donna. "And what have you been doing lately?" she asked.

"I volunteer at Police and Citizens Youth Club, a disco for kids under 12 years of age. Every year I pick up kids in the neighbourhoods so they can go to disco. But this year's disco was the best.

"We had a DJ. The music was deafening, so loud, but I kept dancing with the kids all night long. It brought me back to my younger days when good, old-fashioned music blasted all night long. I was out of step with the rest of the kids, but I didn't care. I just kept on hopping from one foot to another. When Bee-Gees *Staying Alive* came blasting, I put my best dance moves into action.

"Guess what! I got a prize too."

"What did you get?" Valerie asked, grinning.

"A lollipop, of course, just like all the other kids." They

both laughed. "I definitely agree with you, Valerie," Donna said, looking along the table. "We have to keep ourselves looking young, or at least pretend to be young. I have to push myself a little harder to fit in with younger parents to help build happy childhood memories. I don't want my granddaughter to miss out because she lives with an elderly grandparent. I don't want Izzy to feel that she has an old and useless granny."

"Donna, you are the real Dancing Queen," Valerie said, nodding at Donna's comment.

"Thanks, but all the young dancers have wore me out. The following day, I could hardly walk. Every muscle in my body was aching. My disco dancing is over. Next year I'm letting some of the young mums take over from me."

"Yeah, dream on, Donna. Young mums go to the real disco or nightclub while we are stuck at home looking after their kids."

No one missed the sarcasm in Valerie's voice.

Lynne, a lady with her feet firmly on the ground, never ever complained about anything.

"You looked ravishing, Lynne," Donna said, looking at the woman. "I love that flame orange and apricot colour on you. It really suits you. Where did you buy it?"

"At the Salvo Shop … where else? It only cost $10.00, but I had to splurge on my hat and shoes. I must have comfortable shoes as my feet swell in this heat."

"And how is your granddaughter?" Anne asked.

Lynne's eyebrow rose, and she heaved a sigh. "You remember that Simone was doing a cooking apprenticeship? Well, when she finished it, she moved in with her boyfriend and soon fell pregnant."

"How come?" Anne exclaimed.

"The same way we all got pregnant, silly." Lynne smiled.

"Well, the rental got too expensive as there are very few rental homes available. So Simone and her partner and baby Ally all moved back in with us. Because of Covid-19, so many people from the eastern states have wised up to how good it is to live in WA. They are all coming here, as it is the best place to live.

"I have to thank Covid-19 for another baby. Ally is such a gorgeous baby. I love her to bits."

After a collective sigh of "Awww", The Crafty Lot, all thrilled about the new baby, encouraged Lynne to stay positive. It would all sort itself out.

"Covid won't last long," someone in the group mentioned.

"Where is Amelia this year? How come she didn't come? She never misses out on the fun," Valerie asked Penny.

"Amelia went to New South Wales to get to know her other grandkids. Her grandson Phillip left before Covid-19 and started working with his stepdad. He gets along well with his mum and other siblings. Amelia told me that Phillip was getting to know so many stepbrothers and sisters. Phillip is now the most popular sibling among all of them.

"Don't worry. She misses us and will be back after the school holidays."

"Gee! I hope she won't be stuck in quarantine when she lands back in Perth," somebody yelled from the far end of the table."

Penny quickly stepped in with her loud, firm voice. "Listen to you lot! Stop winging. We are lucky to live in the most beautiful and isolated city in the world. "We have hardly noticed that Covid-19 even existed. Our lives and livelihood have hardly been interrupted. We continue to live perfectly normal while Covid-19 has unleashed turmoil and pain on the rest of the world. It's hard to comprehend the enormity of suffering and death in Europe and the US. It seems so unreal, like watching some sort of apocalyptic movie.

"Just look at us, enjoying ourselves here, and the festive season is around the corner. All the restaurants and beaches are packed with happy-go-lucky Aussies."

Nobody could argue with Penny on that.

And Donna definitely agreed. "As a migrant," she said, "I have never taken Australia for granted. And if any of you believe in God, you should know that God himself must have chosen WA as his designated holiday spot on this earth. We truly live in paradise." When she raised her glass to emphasise her statement, the Crafty Lot started clapping.

"What about you, Evelyn?" Tanya was curious to know. "Why did you decide to move to Broome? You look ten years younger now. It must be the misty Tropical climate."

"Covid-19 made me realise that family is the most essential thing in the world. The career that I gave up seems like it was in another lifetime. I have no regrets about leaving that life behind. I've never been happier.

"It was the right decision. Broome is the perfect holiday spot, and we can now be close to our daughter. Our grandkids have finished school and now help their parents on the station, and Allan has a lifetime of experience raising cattle and training racehorses. During the rainy season, he'll help out on the cattle station too, and we can see our grandkids more often.

"Seeing you all today has made me very happy," said Evelyn with a big grin on her face. "It's so relaxing; I am so glad I came."

"Me too, but your tip was not much help. I've lost twenty bucks." Tanya chuckled happily. Then she asked Donna, "How much did you lose?

"I put $10.00 each way on the same horse that Evelyn confidently recommended and lost it too."

Evelyn laughed. She rose and went to the bar and paid for the next round of drinks to compensate for the losses.

The party eventually settled down, the Crafty Lot feeling carefree and maybe a little tipsy. Beverly won $50 in her first Melbourne Cup win ever, and jumped up and down with elation as if she'd won a million. It came as no surprise when Elizabeth won 'the best dressed and the best hat'. She gave her prize, a double movie pass, to Penny for the next fundraiser. The Crafty Lot applauded noisily.

Rhonda was a winner, too. Supporting herself with crutches and, with the apron still wrapped around her waist, she went to collect her winnings. As she opened her bag to stash in her money, a prawn fell out of her 'doggie bag'. Rhonda skillfully stepped on it.

Donna knew now was definitely time to leave the Pub. The party was over.

However, the party actually lasted for another hour, as some stayed on. Others who had obligations started parting ways, saying goodbyes with elbow taps and air kisses. It was the best they could do in those crazy times to give encouragement, love and support.

Penny made sure the taxi mini-van was waiting to take a few of the ladies home, especially those who had overindulged, as sharing the ride kept the cost down. Tanya joined them as she was in a hurry to get home in time to pick up Sienna from pre-school.

As she exited the Pub, she turned around and yelled back, "Donna, see you and Izzy next week at the doggy beach."

"Yeah, sure, next week is going to be hot, and we haven't been to the beach for a while. Call me when you are free."

"Ciao, everyone," Donna waved as she headed out in the other direction. The Crafty Lot waved back.

Evelyn grabbed up her purse and said enthusiastically, "Come on, let me walk with you to the train station so we can have a bit of private catch up."

As two friends casually strolled to the station, chatting happily, Evelyn mentioned in passing, "I'm staying a few more days in Fremantle with my son and his wife. I can't get enough of cuddling my newborn grandson. Besides, I want to do some Christmas shopping while in Perth too.

"Oh, Donna, I can't thank you enough for inviting me to the Melbourne Cup luncheon. It was really lovely catching up with you. I had so much fun today with these happy-go-lucky grandparents. They are such a lively bunch. I had so much fun today. For their ages, they are all so full of life. Tell me, Donna, where on earth have you met so many characters? I haven't laughed like this for ages. Definitely beats our staff parties, don't you agree?" Evelyn said.

"Yeah, I do. And most of them have no choice but to look after their grandkids? You know, there are thousands of grandparents registered with one government organisation or another to receive essential support. And there are probably many more who are not registered – so many quiet achievers that nobody has heard of.

"What is worse, most of the grandparents have to share parental responsibility with the biological parents, with their own children who have mental health issues, alcohol or drug addictions. For the grandparents who are elderly or sick, it creates ongoing conflicts and extra stress.

"Why can't Family Court or DCP give grandparents more support and legal stability for the kids? … because the biological parents and especially mothers are favoured by the system." Donna shook her head, still in disbelief. "Everything is geared toward reconnecting a child with a mother. Mental health issues, domestic violence and drugs are often overlooked."

"But that's not right. When Allan takes his horse to the racetrack in Broome, all the nominated horses have to submit to a drug test. If the horses have drug testing, why aren't mothers drug tested too? The safety of a child should be more critical than a horse race!"

"Oh, Evelyn, you are so naïve." Donna smiled grimly. "I thought so too, but that is not the case. Family law doesn't operate that way. Most grandparents can't afford the legal fees, and the opportunistic lawyers seem to drag out the process year after year, taking advantage of vulnerable and naïve grandparents." She laughed sarcastically. "It's so unfair on the kids? They should remove them from domestic violence and alcohol abuse."

"The last time I heard, drugs were illegal," Evelyn said, somewhat agitated.

"Oh, Evelyn, we can't blame Family Courts." Donna's tone held a hint of sarcasm. "Grandparents are only seen as temporary care. We are not appreciated or valued. To be fair, most of us are too bloody old to take it much further."

She laughed, more out of frustration than the absurdity of it.

"The Family Court is desperately searching to find a long-term solution. It offers biological parents, mediation, consultation, rehabilitation, you name it. The Family Law has to keep biological parents in the game. Connecting children with biological parents keeps the doors open, so kids will have a home when their grandparents die. Besides, the Foster Cares system is overwhelmed as more and more kids need a safe home. And fostering is the last resource."

"The Family Courts can't officially discriminate about old age, but, the indisputable fact is that most grandparents are elderly, and they may not last the distance. Evelyn, my dear friend, there is nothing pleasant about old age, especially when it bites us like this."

"But how come the community or society at large isn't aware of the sacrifices grandparents make?" Evelyn shook her head, to which Donna shrugged.

"It's just terrible that grandparents don't get paid," Evelyn went on. "Donna, you have to petition the government to do something about that. You must get extra funding for these poor grandparents!"

"Huh!" Donna huffed. "Both you and I know that getting extra money is like getting blood out of a stone. Remember at work when we were putting tenders together, it's a tricky business. Getting funding for worthwhile causes is always challenging. There is never enough money to go around. And grandparents always fall to the bottom of that list, relying primarily on charities for support."

"That's not fair," Evelyn replied despondently. "You've all worked and paid taxes like anyone else. You should get more consideration for what you are doing at this time in your life. This is just wrong. So wrong!"

As they were about to enter the train station, Evelyn squeezed Donna in a tight embrace. And Donna thought, *To hell with Covid*, and prolonged the hold. *Sometimes you just need a hug.*

"Now listen," Evelyn said firmly as two friends waited for Donna's train to arrive, "the next school holidays, you, Izzy and Tom must come and visit us in Broome. We have a three-bedroom cottage within walking distance of Cable Beach. I will always have a spare room for you."

"That's great. It looks like I will have my next holiday in Broome," Donna said cheekily.

"Oops! My train is coming. We will catch up in Broome."

"I'll hold you to that." Evelyn hugged her friend as they parted.

"Ciao, Bella. Stay safe," Donna said as she waved goodbye.

As Donna entered the train, she looked around. The train was full of afternoon travellers. Most people's heads were down, trawling through their smartphones, oblivious to their world. The train was packed with students going home from school and universities. There were no seats available.

Donna felt pleasantly surprised when one young student tapped her on the shoulders, offering her his seat. "Wow! Thanks, how nice of you," she responded with a smile.

She sat down and rested her cheek against the warm window. As the train sped away, she thought about those grandparents who brought up this second generation of kids. She looked around at the young people in their different school uniforms and felt optimistic that these young people would inherit the world they lived in.

It will be a wonderful world after all, she thought blissfully.

As soon as Donna arrived home, she joined Tom on the balcony, where he sat reading a book. She carefully started telling Tom all about the individual characters at the party, to which Tom replied, "By the way, did you pick a winning horse?"

"No, but the winnings went to the right person, who needs it more than I do. I got everything that I want right here."

Donna valued every precious moment she spent with Tom and her granddaughter Isabella. They leant on the balcony rail, marvelling at the beauty of the Indian Ocean stretching into the distant horizon. At that instant, she was satisfied with her life and eagerly awaited Izzy arriving home from school.

Soon enough, they heard Isabella's voice and the usual racket as she entered the house on her scooter. Once inside, Isabella called out from downstairs.

"Hello, Nana. I'm home."

Hearing this divine sound, the most beautiful, sweetest voice on this earth, Donna's face beamed with delight.

Izzy dropped the scooter and hurried up the stairs. A moment later, she burst onto the balcony, smiling, her arms outstretched to hug her Nana. After sitting down, Izzy glanced at Donna with pleading eyes.

"Come on, Nana. Let's take Bon-Bon for a walk. Let's go to the dog park. We have lots of fun there."

And so they did.

The Horse Whisperer

The Arts and Craft Group was putting the final touches on all of their handmade Christmas cards. The decorations and gifts were nearly all done. Penny smiled as she counted all the money they had saved and shook a big tin full of coins. Grinning broadly, she praised all their fundraising efforts.

"Ladies, this was a good year. All we have to do now is plan how we are going to spend all this loot." Penny giggled.

"Gail, we all love your cupcakes. Next time, you need to make more cupcakes. They have made us a small fortune," Penny said, grabbing the last one left on the plate and licking her fingers.

The Crafty Lot was especially pleased that all their grandkids would have a wonderful present under their Christmas tree on Christmas day.

"Valerie, what's been happening in your life? You always have some exciting news to share with us," Penny asked.

"Well, on the last long weekend, some of us grandparents with older kids went to Dwellingup camp. One grandmother from another club had a large eight-seated four-wheel drive and a large trailer. Her husband drove, and we all somehow squeezed in.

"We all chucked in sleeping bags, eskies full of food, hot thermos bottles of coffee … with a bit of brandy to keep us warm at night. Dwellingup can get freezing …" Valerie smiled.

Maureen brought two of her great-grandchildren. She's an elder Noongar Aboriginal woman and often takes all of her kids camping.

As soon as we arrived in Dwellingup, Maureen took us on the bush walk to teach the kids about 'bush tucker'. She showed the kids what berries were safe to eat, and what would give them a tummy ache. She said women gathered bush tucker, while the men did the hunting. Maureen also showed the kids how to select bush leaves for medicinal purposes and how to spot kangaroo and possums tracks ... We had a wonderful time exploring the bush.

"When we all got to the river, Maureen showed the kids how Noongar people used to catch fish by using spiked bush branches downstream to trap the fish. The branches made a natural fishing net, and they only took from the water what they needed to eat. It was quite obvious how the Noongar people respected the native fauna and flora. We all learnt that Noongar people lived in harmony with the bush. That was before the white man came and spoiled it all. Now the world has changed and some families fell apart.

"Maureen told us adults how Noongar families looked after each other and how aunties, cousins and extended family members all stuck together ... No wonder her house is always full of kids.

"At nighttime, Maureen showed the kids how to start a fire without matches and then was going to teach them how to make a damper and billy tea, but nobody could light the fire as the floor was wet from the rain."

"Yeah. Lucky for you that I had matches with me," Jenny laughed. "Oh, boy, that was fun. "You should have seen the kids swinging billy tea. Half of it ended up on the ground."

"The kids enjoyed making a real damper and shoving their hands into it. Everybody was so involved cooking on the open fire just the way Aboriginal people did it thousands of years ago," Gail said enthusiastically.

"Oh, yeah … with flour bought from Coles supermarket," Jenny said.

Everybody laughed.

"Maybe so, but it was still fun to make it – making and cooking damper under the stars. Now that was something special our kids will never forget," Gail said.

"Oh, I am sorry I missed it," Donna said. "Next year, when Isabella is older, we will join you too."

"Rhonda came too, but we had to help her a bit. She was still on crutches, and she stayed put looking after our campsite while we explored the bush. Some of the younger mothers were more adventurous and went canoeing in the river. We oldies stayed by the fire sipping what was left of the billy tea from the night before.

"Jenny was showing off, rowing on her canoe faster than the others, but she hit a dead branch and tumbled out and got soaking wet – I think she was trying to impress one of the single dads who shared a cabin next to us.

"No, I wasn't. I told you I hate the man!" Jenny protested.

"Yeah, lucky for you he was a water safety instructor, so he could drag you to safety when you took that tumble into the freezing water. You two shared a fireplace together for quite a while … What was that all about?"

"Ummm … he had some extra brandy to warm my chilled bones?" Jenny explained quickly and then changed the subject. "Yeah, the camp was excellent. We had two cabins, close to the kitchen area and toilets, so the kids didn't have to walk that far during the night.

"The kids had a ball running around the bush, collecting dead wood to light fire at night. The older boys went on the river kayaking with other younger families who volunteered to supervise them in the water. Some of our kids never had fathers, so having some male company while camping was a really wonderful experience for them.

"And some of the older chooks didn't feel like getting wet," Jenny laughed. "It was bloody freezing. But the kids didn't mind falling into the icy river. It was so cold, their teeth were chattering and they were blue in the face. Warming up around the fireplace and turning corn and marshmallows on the fire was the highlight.

"Olivia and Anne brought their grandkids too," Valerie added. "Then, the following day, we all went on a steam train tour through the Jarrah forest. It was exhilarating. Our grandkids really behaved well and other younger parents told us we were doing an excellent job raising our grandkids."

"Yeah, I've been telling you all that for ages," Penny said, laughing. "These young parents don't know how hard grandparents work to bring up their grandchildren. It was good to get such positive feedback."

Valerie put her hand up as to ask permission to speak. "Going to camp was great fun, for the grandparents and our grandkids. We spent four days camping, and all the kids had a wonderful time. Every morning they would go out in the bush with a loaf of bread and feed the kangaroos. Some were hopping around with little joeys. Even the possums weren't scared of coming close to our kids.

"When we returned from the bush walk, the kids had baked potatoes in the coals for dinner, made hot Milo, and sat around the campfire with us oldies. None of them even mentioned iPads or mobile phones," Anne said.

"The bushwalking and all that fresh air were exhausting, and the kids crashed the moment their heads touched the pillow. So we girls could have our coffee and brandy shots," Jenny said. "Now, you girls, don't you talk about me as soon as I turn my back or I will be really cross with you all," she gave them a stern warning.

Gail couldn't wait to tell her story. "Ladies, you'll never believe who we bumped into when we were cooking breakfast at the camping grounds." She looked around the group waiting, then someone said:

"Come on. Stop keeping us guessing?"

"Maria! She was at the same camp with her grandson Adam, and a school minibus full of special needs kids, primary boys with autism. They had booked the cabin further up the hill. Maria had gone along to help the teachers. Kids with autism can be very demanding.

"At first, I didn't recognise her as we haven't seen her since her daughter moved back in to help her. Maria said that she came to the camp as it was wonderful therapy for kids with autism.

"She looked much older and had lost a lot of weight. I wanted to cheer her up so I asked Maria what magic pill she took to lose weight as I needed some – I have tried so many diets, but the fat still rolls around my waist like a Michelin tyre." She laughed.

Valerie then finished her sentence. "Maria told us she was

sick, diagnosed with some sort of overactive thyroid problems."

"I wish I had what she has. Anything to lose some weight, my knees are killing me," Gail said, massaging her swollen knees.

"No way, Gail! You will never lose weight as long as you make these yummy cupcakes," Valerie laughed. "Besides, I'll be jealous if you lose weight. I'll be the biggest in the group.'

Gail gave her one of her sharp looks that would kill. Then she continued.

"Maria hoped that her treatment would be successful but is prepared for the worst. She has looked after Adam for the last twelve years while her daughter went from job to job, never settling down long enough to provide a stable home for Adam. Poor Maria, things are not looking good for her. She must have been desperate to let her daughter move in with her. That will only make things worse, but such is life ….

"Bloody old age. We are all heading that way …," Val said with a shrug.

"Val, stop that nonsense. Nobody from "The Crafty Lot" will get old soon," Jenny exclaimed.

"Anyway, Maria came over to our camp at night when all the kids were asleep. She told us that her husband Carlos wanted some peace and quiet, so he packed his bags and moved back to Majorca, Spain, where his family owns a Bed and Breakfast. She couldn't go with him because she had to take care of her autistic grandson. We sat by the fire with a hot cuppa with a dash of brandy, you know, to keep us warm … did I mention it gets freezing cold at night?"

"Oh, I was freezing. Luckily I took a hot water bottle to warm my feet at night," Valerie replied.

Then Jenny went on. "The following day, we met an extraordinary lady. Karyn woke everybody up before breakfast as she drove into the camp area in a huge muddy truck with a massive trailer attached to it. The trailer had two horses, two ponies, a few goats, sheep, ducks, and chickens in it. Some blokes stepped up and helped her to assemble a fence for all the animals.

By the time we cooked breakfast, our camp and the bush next to the river had been converted into a farmyard."

"I learned something new …" Valerie told the ladies.

"What was that?" Gail said, laughing. "I thought you knew everything."

"Oh, stop picking on me. Wait until I tell you. Okay … Karyn is a horse whisperer. These horses could communicate with her. I couldn't believe my eyes when Karyn started helping autistic kids to talk to her horses.

"All the kids who had autism felt so at ease, and not at all scared. Horses must have some sixth sense or something, especially when they are surrounded by kids with disabilities.

"Karyn was so patient with the kids. When our grandkids stood around watching, Karyn invited them all in, just a few at a time so as not to spook the horses. The kids had a ball, feeding goats, cuddling goats and chasing chickens and ducks around, and it helped our kids become involved with the autistic kids. Some of the younger kids went on a pony ride, too. Dwellingup Camp will never be the same after that experience. All the kids had so much fun.

"A few dads from other cabins came down to the riverside camp to help lift kids on the horse saddles further up the hill. It was great to see all these younger dads helping out. All the kids had a horse ride, something so exciting and new," Gail added passionately. "I was so impressed.

"My Justin was too scared to go on the big horse, but Karyn reassured him that she would take care of the horse. She told Justin, 'The horses listen to me, they trust me, we are best of friends. Horses never disappoint, and are obedient. That can't be said for some people,' and she gave him a wink. So Justin and the other boys went on a horse ride along the river, not frightened because Karyn held the horse's reins in her hand. The horses listened to her as she whispered in their ears. They even put their heads down so she could talk to them.

"Yeah, and Karyn is right: talking to horses is easy, but talking with people is much harder. It's no wonder that some kids feel safer with horses than with some of their own parents."

"Well, our group and other campers invited Karyn to share a meal with us around the bonfire. She told us she only does a few camps a year, volunteering mainly for kids with special needs. Horses have a special kind of magic; they know how we feel before we do. And connecting kids with animals has a therapeutic effect on them, especially for kids with autism.

She said she'd been working with horses all her life, and they were such gentle, sensitive animals. She has great-grandkids that love going to her farm, and like her, her children and her grandchildren love to play with the horses.

"Yeah, the camp was great. And watching Karyn and the kids with the horses and ponies was a unique experience. All the kids had a ball ..."

"Yeah, and they still hadn't asked for their mobile phones or iPads," Anne said, laughing.

"The kids sat with us at night around the fire, and you could feel they were comfortable around us oldies."

"It must have been all that Horse Whispering magic," someone laughed.

"In the late afternoon," Valerie went on, "everybody helped dismantle the fence, and all the animals were safely loaded back in the trailer. Then Karyn joined us for a cup of tea. She owns a farm in Waroona, only a few kilometres from Dwellingup, and invited us to drop in at her farm the next time we come to Dwellingup camp. She told us springtime is the best time as the wildflowers are all over the paddock, in purples, blues, yellows, and all the colours of the rainbow."

"That would be great," Penny responded.

"And Karyn said it will not cost us anything," Valerie said with some urgency.

"Oh, yes, it will," Gail contradicted her. "I promised to make some more cupcakes. I made two dozen cupcakes for Dwellingup camp. But if we go to Karyn's farm next spring, I will have to make at least double that amount. She's an amazing woman … it will be a pleasure to make a double load.

"When she heard we were Grandparent carers, Karyn told us her story as we sat around the fire with a cup of tea. She and her husband, Fred, breed what she called 'performance' horses. That's horses for sport – showjumpers and dressage horses mainly. Even so, her story is the same as most of us."

"What do you mean?" Donna's head lifted with interest.

"Karyn is going through the Family Court to get visitation rights to see her two great-grandkids. Bloody shocking if you ask me.

"Her oldest daughter is a lawyer, and she turned against her own mother, advising her daughter not to allow her two kids to spend any time with their great-grandmother on her farm."

"It all started when Karyn informed the kid's biological fathers that they needed to intervene as the kids were being neglected and abused by their mother and that her granddaughter was in a relationship with a real nasty bloke. Drugs, alcohol and domestic violence, and the kids were getting hurt."

"Karyn joined forces with the kids' fathers as she wanted to protect these two little kids who she is very close to. So the dads and she went together to the Family Court.

"She was close to tears when she told us that, a few weeks ago, when she picked her great-grandchildren up to stay with her at the farm for a few days, poor little Tommy had bruises all over his legs. He wanted to stay with Karyn, telling her, 'Gran, I don't want to go home. Mummy will hurt me', and seven-year-old Krista was too frightened to be around mum's new boyfriend. She wanted to go and live with her Gran, too.

"You can imagine, Karyn was getting upset and agitated as she told us this. She said that her granddaughter was incapable of providing a safe home for kids. All she wanted was to party and have a good time with her new boyfriend, which usually meant getting drunk. Her kids were her meal tickets. She wants to keep them to get single mothers' pension."

"Haven't we heard that before!" Donna piped in.

"Karyn told us she got in touch with the kids' fathers, who both have new partners and seem to live decent lives. Then all hell broke loose. Karyn's own daughter, who won't step in to protect her grandchildren, has turned against her, accusing Karyn of not being loyal. She is now fighting with her in the Family Court.

"But Karyn said she would not give up, no matter what; she has to put her great-grandkids first, before her own daughter and granddaughter too. She's an amazing lady to do that," Gail said, protective of this new friend they had made at camp.

"I've seen adults fighting a battle on the back of these poor, innocent children," Donna said, getting quite agitated. "Playing dirty games against each other, just to be spiteful, with the poor kids right in the middle. These so-called adults should be ashamed of themselves, sacrificing the well-being of these poor kids just to hurt the other person. It is criminal … and often, poor kids end up as collateral damage."

Thankfully, Valerie said, "The Family Court has finally given Karyn permission to see her great-grandchildren once a forthright. Karyn has to drive two hours to pick them up and two hours to drop them back. The kids can't wait to stay at Karyn's farm and the little ones are learning to ride the ponies. They love it there, playing with the animals and getting dirty. I guess that's all part of the fun of being on a farm. And what more can you want for kids.

"Why would any mother not let her kids enjoy such freedom, to be spoiled and loved by great-grandparents?" Gail was still upset over it.

"Sad isn't it," Donna said. "From my own experience, I

can tell you that it's unforgivable what some adults put kids through. They should be bloody locked up, punished for causing emotional and physical harm to a child."

Anne lifted her glass of water. "One day, Karyn's great-grandkids will remember that time they spent on that farm. I'm sure these special memories will be remembered as the best part of their childhood. Hooray for Karyn. She fights for her great-grandkids, just like we all do."

"Well, I must say," Valerie took back the lead in the conversation, "this Camp was one of the best adventures our kids have had. And all the animals, especially the horses, have been such a highlight for all the kids. I can't wait to visit Karyn's farm and would be more than happy to make the ton of cupcakes."

"Yes, Gail, we all love your cupcakes. You could open a business and make a small fortune."

"Oh, no, she won't," Penny stepped in. "If we plan to go camping and visit Karyn's farm with our grandkids, there is no time to lose. We have to start fundraising early. Next week, when we get our stall at the Sunday markets, we can start selling some of our Christmas cards. They are all unique, and we've got some children's books that were donated …

"And Maureen's aboriginal dot-paintings always make us good money. She has painted a few good-sized paintings that will get us some decent money."

"Yeah. I buy one this year too," Donna said excitedly. "Maureen is so patient, putting dot after dot. In the end, it is all connected, perfect balance and harmony. I love Aboriginal painting … it is so spiritual and exquisite."

"Hey, don't forget Gail's cupcakes. They always sell like

hotcakes," Jenny said.

"Gail cupcakes make us the most money; she's our best fundraising machine."

"Yes, we all love your cupcakes. You can open a business and make a small fortune. Any other suggestions you might have," Penny asked.

Cheers came all around.

"Okay. We all agreed: we are going to Karyn's farm this springtime. I am looking forward to meeting her. She's a great-grandmother. She is one of us … Besides, I've never met a horse whisperer," Penny said happily.

Free Lunch and a Basket of Ironing

Donna was worried that the sudden downpour of rain would make driving quite hazardous. The day was chilly too, but she was getting ready to go regardless. Rushing around, she prepared Isabella's school lunch so she could get her to school on time when the phone rang.

"Hi, Donna. Are you still going to the seminar at the university?" Jackie asked.

"Yeah. I got the invite at the last minute, most probably because somebody could not attend. It will have a few prominent politicians and VIP guests. We may learn something new."

"I agree. This may be something different. The WA State Government Report on the Grandparent carers will finally come into print. It will be interesting." Jackie replied. "Now listen, Donna, I am happy to drive … I have a few more invites, so I informed Tanya and Penny. I will pick them up first. Wait for me outside."

"Thanks, Jackie, that will be great. I hate driving while raining. The weather prognoses are not looking good. It will be much less stressful for me."

"Yeah, don't worry. It will be much easier if I drive – I've still got my student parking pass from that university where I completed my postgraduate studies in social studies."

Jackie was right on time and familiar with how to get to the university. Soon the group was filled with anticipation of what to expect from the day's seminar.

"Jackie, how did you get so many invitations?" Tanya asked.

"Through the back door, where else? I worked for the mental health department as a counsellor-psychologist and attended many seminars as part of my professional development. But this one is the one I was waiting for.

"But I wouldn't be surprised if they have blacklisted me."

"Why would they do something like that?" Penny asked with an uncertain laugh.

"I don't get easily intimidated, and speak my mind. I ask delicate questions, not politically correct ones. I've annoyed politicians by asking questions they couldn't find answers to." Jackie laughed. "I think they are glad that I became a primary carer for my granddaughter and retired earlier than planned."

"I didn't know you had to retire too," Tanya cut in.

"Yeah. It was challenging to manage my home life and my career. I quit my job a few years ago when Hannah came to live with us. I've seen so many kids turn to drugs or homeless during my working career because of family breakdowns."

"I can't imagine you not working." Donna looked up.

"Yeah, me too," she laughed. "I now do volunteer workshops, but only for Grandcarers who are raising teenagers who are suffering from mental health illnesses.

"My Dave couldn't manage without me there. He has diabetes, so I had no choice but to quit. Hannah is our priority; she will be a teenager soon. That's when grandparents need to be extra careful. It's difficult dealing with hormonal changes and bad moods. We have to be extra patient. I used to work for DCP, and their policy is to reunite families. I never imagined that I would be one of these grandparents fighting against that same system one day. I hated the bureaucracy. That's why I still do volunteer work. I want to help grandparent carers."

The women applauded Jackie's efforts.

"Besides, I am kept busy running around with Hannah. She still has post-traumatic stress, witnessing and living with domestic violence. We finally brought some stability into her life. Her confidence has improved and she's just started acting and making movies. That will help her improve her low self-esteem and come out of her shell."

"That must be very expensive. How do you manage?" Tanya asked.

"It's difficult on a pension, but we manage. I got some funding approved from *iDareDream*. They place emphasis on helping children by paying for schoolbooks, sports or other activities. I will give you the number so you can contact the charity director if you like. The charity organisation understands our plight."

"So exactly what is this seminar all about?" Donna wanted to know.

"The government has finally done some research and acknowledged that Grandparent carers actually exist. Years overdue, but it is finally here."

"It's about time. Who knows, some changes may happen now," Tanya said wistfully.

"Well, let's wait and see. Don't count your chickens. Not just yet." Jackie still had reservations.

"Grandparent carers are the last thing on the government's list."

"Do you think this will ever change?" Donna asked.

"I don't think so. The Seminar will probably be one big show. I've seen it all before."

"I can't wait to ask why grandparents can't get paid like foster parents do," Penny said enthusiastically.

"Ha! That will never happen, and that's because most of us grandparents feel a moral obligation to help our grandkids. Blood is thicker than water, and we love our grandkids. They know we will do it for free. So why would any government pay us any money to support them? But I can tell you one thing …" Jackie continued, "they didn't want me to attend this seminar, voicing my opinions because I may ask questions that the Member of Parliament will have to avoid answering.

"I've also heard that some grandparents from the northern suburbs were selected to make speeches in front of the dignitaries and local government representatives …" Jackie sounded disappointed about that.

Knowing her way around the university campus, Jackie parked close to the entrance to avoid getting wet. The women wanted to leave an excellent first impression, and the rain would have ruined their hair and meticulously applied make-up.

The entrance hall looked welcoming. Visitors were greeted warmly and given name badges and a glossy official report. Jackie led the way as they were ushered straight into a convention room and assigned back row seating. The last rows of chairs were so far from the podium, as far as possible from where the VIP guests and dignitaries were already seated.

Donna looked around, thinking, *Jackie is right …*

overlooked precisely for the reason that she stated. Her questions would have been inappropriate, intimidating some government representatives. It looks like the Grandparents will not get the answers that we were hoping to get. Not today.

The chatter soon stopped when the Master of Ceremony stepped up to the podium and commenced the proceedings with an acknowledgment to the first nation custodians of the land and local elders then welcomed everybody. After the official anthem, government MP and VIP guest speakers were introduced. The official proceeding was on its way.

As the speakers presented different topics about Grandparent carers' and official research, applause followed the many promises made. They acknowledged that Grandparent carers were the hidden population and the fastest growing form of out-of-home care for vulnerable children in Australia. Emphasis was given to recognising Grandparent carers' sacrifices, and acknowledgment and respect came from every speaker. However, most of the Grandcarers had heard this rhetoric many times before. Nothing had ever changed. Some of the grandparents seated in the back rows started fidgeting or pretended to read the information in the colourful, glossy magazine. Some turned the pages to pass the time, only half-listening as speakers continued their acknowledgments and praise from the podium of the Grandparent carers' efforts.

What grandparents needed to hear was that more financial support from the Federal Government would be forthcoming. Some VIP speakers identified a lack of policies that directly affected grandparent carers and their grandchildren, recognising that the legal system had made no significant changes since it was brought to life in 1975.

It was still full of red-tape bureaucracy to properly administer child protective services. VIP speakers talked about the lack of health or education services, promises and support made with childcare subsidies, inadequate housing, and unattainable expensive rental accommodation. The report concluded that the new Advisory Groups would research the project further. In addition, the grandparent carers would be asked to actively take part in shaping some new governing policy.

At the end of the seminar, the focus was on interviewing a few selected Grandcarers who spoke of their own personal struggles. None of the grandparents asked troublesome questions, and random questions from the audience weren't on the agenda, either. The seminar had to stick to the scheduled timetable. Random questions from the audience were not encouraged, and Jackie and her friends had no opportunity to express their opinions publicly or ask questions of the presenters.

It soon became apparent to Donna that Jackie wasn't cynical in her thinking as she observed handpicked grandparents from the northern part of the city. Her heart thudded dully. *It's blatantly obvious these politically correct questions and answers have been rehearsed.* Even one indigenous grandparent was included in the presentation via Zoom. She looked around as the previously silent audience started applauding the event organisers.

No government will tackle such a big issue as us. It would take a major miracle to lower grandparents' financial burden. It just won't happen. Donna shook her head, deflated.

Most of the invisible Grandcarers were relieved when the show was over.

Jackie was the first to jubilantly jump from her seat. She stretched and yawned. "Hooray, girls, let's go. It is time for lunch."

Everyone rushed out. The aroma of percolated coffee was enticing, and the lunch spread terrific, a variety of freshly baked savoury snacks, sweets, and Danish pastries, followed by warm pumpkin scones and tons of cream, served with freshly brewed coffee and the finest tea.

Jackie joined the group and whispered: "Just look around. Most government representatives have disappeared, supposedly rushing to attend another pressing engagement. They skipped the lunch, just in case some of us eager grandparents bombard them with one-on-one questions. Run, run, run as fast as they can."

Jackie and her group laughed.

"I don't intend to attend any more of these gatherings. It's a bloody waste of petrol."

"At the end of the year, there will be another meeting at Parliament House. Is anybody going?" Jackie asked.

"I am not interested anymore. I am sick and tired of listening to these politicians promising but never delivering," was the common response.

"After COVID-19, they promised to increase the grandparent carer once a year payment. But we are still waiting. The Federal Government is wasting money on everything, including building new submarines, and every budget so far has completely overlooked the Grandparent carers' plight."

Tanya rushed to get an oversized plate to fill with delicious selections of dishes. She turned around and whispered: "Ladies, if the spread of food is as good as this,

I may attend. Parliament House has a big budget for entertainment. We could all go just to get free lunch."

"Yeah, and disappear just like today's MP has done to us today," Janice giggled, her sarcasm still present.

"Just look at the food. It must have cost a small fortune, and the venue hire would be expensive too. It would have been better if some of that money was given to us to purchase school books for our grandkids," Penny said.

"Yes, that would have been more helpful. But this seminar had a special purpose too," Jackie reminded them.

"What was that?" Donna frowned with confusion.

"It will keep us grandparents quiet for another year."

"Oh, Jackie, don't be so negative? Something might eventually happen," Penny tried to stay positive.

"Ho-hum … I've heard all these promises so many times before, I have absolutely no illusion on what it's all about. But the food is good." Jackie laughed.

Another hour was spent chatting, meeting with other grandparents and half-listening while selecting different goodies from the buffet table. Food indeed was the only reward that day.

No matter how much effort and sacrifices grandparents made, they would never be fully appreciated and valued. No monetary contributions for their services would ever be forthcoming. The story kept repeating itself time and time *again*.

Like the cyclic skipping of an LP vinyl record. Donna repeated in her mind.

The Grandparent carers didn't just struggle with role identity and conflict as the new parents of their grandchildren, they also experienced social isolation, fewer financial resources, and less physical stamina than younger parents, as well as unexpected and growing health problems.

For many grandparents, this seminar was one of many. Nothing much resonated with the grandparents, except for some who shook hands with a VIP guest. Many photos were taken – smiles all around, and everybody was happy. It seemed.

And the show was over…

Driving back home, Jackie put on her foot down slightly to be on time to pick the kids up from school. She was still quite outspoken, even the food not completely quelling her angst.

"Ladies, don't expect miracles. Grandparent carers should stop hoping for better times ahead after this meeting. The promises and pledges were only to sweeten us up, like candy to children, and to keep us quiet for a while. Don't be fooled by this political curtain-raiser. And the seminar was timed well too. Have you noted that there's a federal election on the horizon? Today was just another show of self-promotion, nothing more."

Donna understood Jackie's bitterness. She was disillusioned and angry with the system too.

Jackie still had to attend Family Court hearings, fighting a bureaucracy that was reluctant to randomly test her daughter for drugs. She only wanted what was in the best interest of her granddaughter.

"How are you progressing with your Interim Court Orders?" Donna asked her one day.

"The Family Court is putting up with my daughter's refusal to have a drug test. She gave so many false promises to get rehabilitated. But they are all but empty words." Jackie shrugged. "It's a tough battle when you have to face the biological mother. I love my daughter, but I love my granddaughter more.

"My daughter has drug problems and mental health issues and is the whole cause of the problem, yet she gets free legal aid and we have to pay." She groaned and blew out a breath. "I get so irritable with such an unjust system. It sickens me that her non-compliance to Court Order is tolerated by the Family Court. I've seen so much bullshit and red tape, it drives me crazy."

"Dave and I are worried sick that Hannah will end up back with her mother. It's not fair, is it? We don't know what to do?" She sounded defeated.

"Whatever you do, Jackie, don't give up," Donna encouraged her. "Don't give up. For Hannah's sake. You do still have one ace card in your hands. So stick with that one thing that is going to get you across the line."

"What's that?"

"Well, my dear, drugs are illegal. The Family Court can't get around that? So don't give an inch. Agree on supervised visits only. Stay strong. The law must be on your side. We all know that drugs are illegal. And Tom and I learned one lesson the hard way. It was a very costly lesson. Don't make the same mistakes," Donna stated firmly.

"What's that? I can do with some good news," Jackie responded.

"Don't waste your money on lawyers. They all work together. The aim is always to engage the biological mother to actively be involved as a parent, the fathers, however, are mostly ignored. Grandparents are temporary solutions, probably because we are too old. We've all heard that one."

"I only care that my granddaughter is safe," Jackie almost growled. "But the ICL is pushing us to give my daughter more access time with Hannah. I know my daughter better than he does. Hannah once ended up in hospital black and blue when her mother didn't have enough dope and lost control. At the Family Court, this incident is all but forgotten now, and the ICL is still pushing us to give her unsupervised contact. He doesn't listen to our concerns. I won't allow Hannah to be abused or hurt by her mother. Not now. Not ever." Jackie's voice trembled now as her anger grew.

"Whatever we say, the lousy system wants to give my daughter so many more chances. One time, Dave got so upset and stressed that his blood pressure went through the roof. He's got a pacemaker, so I was worried about him. He is sick and tired of going back and forth to mediation meetings and conferences. Nothing ever works!

"Next week, we are back in the Family Court again, and I'll spend half of my superannuation fighting a battle that we can't win. My daughter still refuses to have a drug test. We are still dancing to her tune. What do you think I should do, Donna?"

"You are an innovative, intelligent, and capable woman. You can represent yourself. Don't waste any money on those crooked, greedy lawyers. Stay strong, Jackie. It will all work out in the end. Don't give in, no matter how hard the ICL is trying to convince you. His job is supposed to be to protect the child. That's his title: ICL — Independent Children's lawyer. You must insist on a drug test. No tests, no visits. Simple as that. This is in the best interests of your granddaughter. Protect your granddaughter."

At this point, Tanya stepped into the conversation. "We had similar problems with the Family Court. It is so stressful for many grandparents. My husband was going through a tough time with his chemotherapy. He was in complete remission for nearly two years. But his cancer returned. It was all due to the stress."

"That's the way things are?" Penny said, rationalising.

"I know it is hard, but the grandparents have to stay strong," Donna stated. "We had the same problem. Everything was done to appease the biological mother. She produced no drug tests, and our family matter dragged on for nearly five years. But we never agreed on unsupervised visits. Eventually, we signed a consent order, where we decided that Izzy's mother could come and see her any time in consultation with us. But she never did, and I don't expect that this will change soon."

"Yeah," Tanya said. "I have to agree with you. Grandparents will never be treated equally. My oldest granddaughter will finish high school at the end of this year, and suddenly her father wants her to come and live with him. I had to let her go. My heart is broken. I have no choice in the matter."

The weather had now improved, and the sun was out again. Going home to cook dinner for their grandkids was all they could think about it now. They each put into practice their motto: Take one day at a time. That was all that mattered.

The following week, Donna received an invite to attend another meeting at the Parliament House. On that occasion, there were more VIPs and MPs. Only five grandparent carers attended. Some may have stayed home because of Covid-19. It was a nice sunny day so some may have opted to do some weeding in the garden, washing up or even attempt to do the ironing. Everything was better than listening to politicians talking, mostly about themselves. The next day, Donna checked the front page of the prominent WA newspaper to see if anything was written about the grandparent's plight. It had photos of the upcoming football grand final clash. Football fever was in the air, so the pages were reserved for analysing game strategies; photos of footy stars splattered all over the front page.

The middle pages we reserved for political self-promotions' and upcoming federal elections. The grandparent's seminar didn't warrant a mention in the small print either.

Donna remembered when Jackie told her she would rather do ironing than attend another seminar. When she returned home that afternoon from Parliament House, she looked at her ironing basket and thought, *I wish I had stayed home and done some ironing. It would have been less painful, and definitely more productive.*

Christmas Picnic for the Grandparents

Another day, while doing Christmas shopping at the local shops, Donna bumped into Jackie and the two friends decided to stop for a cappuccino and a chat at Miss Maud's.

"Donna, are you going to the Kings Park picnic organised for grandparents who are caring for their grandchildren next week?"

"I know nothing about that. Tell me more."

"The picnic is sponsored and organised by a charity organisation called *iDareDream* that supports and focuses mainly on children. Everybody will come; bring Isabella too. It will be fun for kids. Pack a picnic basket, and I will pick you up next Sunday."

"Of course, I will join you. I wouldn't want to miss anything organised for the children." Donna smiled.

*****

The following Sunday, Jackie and her granddaughter Hannah arrived on time. Tanya and her granddaughter Sienna sat in the back, and Izzy jumped in the middle between the two girls. Donna helped Jackie pack the picnic chairs, a table, snacks, junk food, a cooler full of soft drinks, and water to keep them cool, as it was a scorching day.

Donna jumped in the passenger seat next to Jackie once packed and ready to leave.

"Okay, kids, are you excited that we are going to Kings Park? Santa will bring you a heap of presents," Jackie said to assure the children that the day would be filled with games and fun activities.

"Yeah!!!" the girls screamed excitedly and happily settled back to play with their iPad.

"Who funds that charity?" Donna wanted to know again.

"Virginia started the organisation and gets funding from local businesses. She wants to help kids to do more sports and other fun activities. I've already got some money from the *iDareDream* charity for Hannah's dancing lessons. Today, you will meet Virginia; she's so passionate about helping kids and has done a lot of running around putting this Christmas picnic together."

"Do you have to register to become a member?" Donna wanted to know.

"Yes, the registration only costs $10. I was told that I could bring a few grandparent carers with me today."

As soon as they had parked, Jackie greeted another grandmother and introduced her arrivals.

"Hi, Rosanne. Glad you came early. This is the best spot."

"Please, ladies, make yourself comfortable. I made extra salads and cold meats. My three kids are running around, but they will soon be hungry. I've got so much leftover food, so please help yourselves." Rosanne pointed at her picnic table.

The grandparents settled in and set up the picnic adding more salads, cold meats, chips, and water. The kids didn't waste any time and quickly became acquainted with the other children and started exploring the playground, climbing, and jumping on the swings and play equipment.

Jackie introduced Virginia, who warmly greeted everyone. She was busy running around with a few of her volunteers, helping to make the Christmas celebration a special occasion for all.

Jackie brought the ice cream, and it felt so refreshing on such a hot day in the lush bushland in King's Park. Ladies relaxed and chatted among themselves. Donna was surprised to see how many grandparents attended.

"Jackie, just look around you," Rosanne said at one point. "The whole picnic ground is full of grandparents and their kids. When you see them all congregated together, you realise just how many grandparents are engaged in raising their grandchildren."

Donna stood up and walked around the picnic grounds; she looked around at the blankets that spread so far across the park. "I never imagined there were so many of us." When she sat down and started nibbling on some salad, she looked around again.

"How many grandparents come to a picnic? It must be around one hundred or more."

It was a sheer joy watching the children play; children full of energy; children with bubbly personalities. Happy, playful kids. Grandparents looked like normal younger parents, lovingly watching their grandchildren having fun. The Christmas picnic at the King's Park celebration stretched all afternoon.

As they settled back into their portable picnic chairs, a young boy and his twin sister arrived all puffed out. He grabbed a handful of chips.

"Nana, can we have some drinks, please?" said another

child running towards Rosanne.

Rosanne pulled soft drinks out of her esky. Then a few minutes later, another sweet little girl, a toddler, came running, crying as she'd fallen and scraped her knees.

"Mama, Mama," she cried.

Rosanne gently cuddled and comforted the little girl, and wiped her tears. "Don't worry, sweetie, Mama will kiss it better."

It worked, and the toddler smiled and ran off to catch up with the older siblings at the playground.

"How come she calls you mama, and the other two grandchildren call you nana?" Donna again, curious.

"The youngest one, Suzie, is from another father. We got her when she was one year old. My little Suzie just turned three, and she has only known me as her mum, so she calls me mama."

"How many adult kids do you have?" Jackie asked.

"Well, I got four adult children. Three of them turned out to be my pride and joy. These days that is good odds. Don't you think so? Sadly, my youngest daughter got involved with the wrong crowd, which led to drugs.

"She's in Sydney, and I hope she stays there. We had to spend a small fortune to get the two oldest kids to come and live with us in WA. DCP called us to come and get her just in time before the Covid-19 restrictions came and interrupted our travel plans. Then my daughter signed the temporary consent orders, and now Suzie lives with us, too. Thank God for Covid-19; my daughter won't be able to visit us soon. And when she does, she will only bring us more trouble. I hope the borders stay close for good. That would suit me just fine," Rosanne concluded.

The Kings Park picnic was a lovely day indeed. The fresh, slightly hot air at King's Park and the natural environment created the perfect ambience, Donna thought. And it gave grandparents a chance to sit and mix in a leisurely way while their kids were running around the playground.

When everyone had finished eating, the organisers gathered all the children in one place and encouraged them to sit patiently, waiting with great anticipation for Santa to arrive from the lush green bush full of bottlebrush plants and flowering shrubs.

Tanya jumped up enthusiastically and grabbed a bottle of cool water to greet Santa, turning around and telling everybody: "Oh, my God, I feel so sorry for poor Santa. He must be so hot, delivering presents for our grandkids on such a scorching day."

The party came to a stop when the chubby man in red arrived, and all the kids gathered around to receive their gifts. The grandparents didn't miss out either, each receiving a box of chocolate. That was the highlight of the day for all the kids and young-at-heart grandparents.

Everyone was thankful for such a lovely day that the *iDareDream* charity organised for grandparent carers and their grandchildren.

Donna thought: *If only she could bottle that moment in time. Life seems to be so perfect.*

*****

Rosanne offered Donna and Izzy a home lift as the day was winding down. They realised they didn't live so far apart and it saved Jackie having to go out of her way. On the way home, they stopped at the beach so the children could have an ice cream and a quick swim too. The picnic at Kings Park had been great, but it had also been an extremely hot day.

"I was so surprised that so many grandparents came to a Kings Park picnic," Donna admitted.

"That is only the tip of the iceberg," Rosanne chuckled. "In a few weeks, we will go to another Christmas celebration. You should come with me next fortnight, for the end-of-year celebration. It's quite a long drive north of the river, and you can meet many more grandparent carers. A few hundred usually turn up at the end of the year celebrations."

"Where is it?" Donna asked.

"Somewhere up north of the river. That organisation is much more significant. It's called Grandparents Rearing Grandchildren WA.".

"Who is the organiser of that?"

"Grandparents Raising Grandchildren WA. It's run by grandparent volunteers too and is supported by local businesses," Rosanne explained. "Jan has been involved for years. This year she won a Senior Citizens' WA award. You must come with me. The kids always have such fun on that barbecue afternoon."

"Yeah, but that is such a long drive," Donna responded.

"Don't worry, my van seats eight, so there is plenty of room for you. I will pick another grandparent with two of her grandkids, too. You don't have to bring anything. It will be all provided by the organisation. The kids will get another Christmas present too.

"Last year, even Santa was surprised to see so many kids in one spot. It is always heaps of fun and has a carnival atmosphere, just like a sports carnival. Volunteers, mostly elderly granddads, man the sausage sizzle and cremate the chops. Grandmothers prepare fruit salads and sweets for kids. The best part of the barbecue is there is no washing up."

Donna was convinced. "Okay, that would be lovely. Izzy will be excited to see all her little friends again. Thanks for picking me up."

A few weeks later, the friends gathered for that Christmas celebration. The moment Rosanne parked her van, Donna jumped out of the car and, in a bouncy step, found another acquaintance, a middle-aged woman who had secured a shady spot under the huge eucalyptus tree.

"Hi, Yvonne. I am glad you were here early to pick us the best spot. I can see so many familiar faces already," Rosanne said as she hugged her friend.

Donna instantly noticed the most striking thing: how many more grandparents assembled in the park, so many more than she could ever have imagined. Grandparents of all ages played and interacted with each while their grandchildren ran around making new friends and burning off energy. There were so many grey-headed grannies. Some supported themselves with walking sticks, while other younger grandparents with more energy ran around and played games with their grandchildren.

Donna thought, *If an outsider looked, it would be deceived only by the age of these parents. Such a lovely lazy day.*

As several grandparents joined them at the park picnic table, somebody in the group asked, "Yvonne, how is your husband doing?"

"He's finished his chemotherapy and is doing well. We are optimistic that he will soon go into complete remission. Keeping the borders shut is really good for us. My husband is immune-compromised. We are worried that he may get Covid-19 when the W.A. borders open up."

"Yeah, I feel for you. Many elderly grandparents who have underlying health conditions are worried about getting Covid-19," Jackie agreed. "Right now, it feels good to be so isolated, so we can stay healthy."

Rosanne smiled and nodded vigorously. "It feels good to have peace of mind that I can keep my grandkids. I don't know how long that will last because we only have interim orders. We will probably have to go back to court when the borders open.

"My husband's a FIFO – works up north in mines and earns good wages. He was planning on retiring early, but lawyers are costly, so he will have to stay at work till this is all over," she said.

"It must be hard to raise three grandchildren. Do you have any support from other members of your family?" Tanya asked.

"Yeah, it is difficult, but I have a big family here. My two daughters live here in Perth and help as much as possible. It's our youngest daughter who lives in Sydney that has made all of our lives miserable."

"I still work part-time as a nurse at the Fiona Stanley Hospital. Luckily, they know my home situation at work, so I only get the shifts when the kids are at school. But school holidays are much harder to manage."

"We can help with babysitting, especially during school holidays," Donna suggested.

"I am so surprised that so many grandparents came to the picnic. There are so many of us?" Yvonne commented.

Everything was so well organised again that the day was indeed a memorable experience for all the grandparents and their grandchildren.

*****

A few weeks later, Jackie phoned, excited. "I will pick you up next week. Everybody is coming along with grandkids, so you are coming too," Jackie stated firmly.

"Where are we going this time?" Donna grinned at her enthusiasm.

"The end-of-year celebration at the science museum – Sci-Tech in Perth. It's organised by WANSLEA. That is the most prominent organisation of all and offers support to WA Grandcarers. It will be great for the kids. The whole museum is booked just for the grandparents who are raising grandchildren.

"I will pick you up at 5 pm. Supper will be provided too. The best part, no dishes to be washed here either."

"Okay. I will be ready," Donna laughed.

True to her word, Jackie was on time, and they all squeezed into her van. The drive to the city was easy, too. After 5 pm, most people were already home, and the freeway was not that crowded.

When they arrived, the cafeteria area was already chocked full of grandparents. Kids of all ages were scattered throughout the centre experimenting with science projects.

Rosanne warmly welcomed all other grandparents at the reserved tables, as there were hardly any free spaces available. Yvonne brought another newcomer grandparent that joined the group that day, and she also brought along a bucket full of lollies and chocolates for her two kids to share with all the other grandkids. There was so much food and sweets spread out on the buffet table.

Hundreds of kids of all ages immersed themselves in exciting scientific gadgets and science experiments. The rowdy group of women started chatting together, all at ease. Some husbands came too, enjoying club sandwiches and cupcakes and sipping cups of tea, relaxing knowing that the kids were well looked after and safe.

"Yvonne, why do your grandkids call you by your first name?" somebody asked.

"Oh, I am far too young to be a grandmother, let alone be called Grandma. So I told my grandkids to call me Yvonne. The little one still calls me Yves, but they call my husband Poppy."

She sighed. "I miss the old life. I never expected I'd become a primary carer for my grandchildren. I was a bank manager working in the finance sector and loved interacting with clients. It was rewarding. Now I only work a few days a week as a cashier. I wasn't prepared for this new lifestyle. Don't get me wrong … I love my grandchildren, but what choice did I have?" Yvonne concluded, looking despondent.

Donna stood and walked around the venue, watching the children, watching the grandparents as they lovingly took photos with their grandkids. How often she had heard the plight of grandparents, and Rosanne's story was so close to her own. When she rejoined the group, she said as she sat down with her cup of coffee:

"To see so many grandparents all in one place is an eye-opener. It is good to know that I am not alone anymore. Meeting so many new friends in similar situations is comforting. This venue was a perfect choice. Best place to be," she remarked.

"It is great that the grandparents and grandchildren are together under the same roof. And it's lovely to spend some time with you, ladies. I think I will come to a few more meetings next year."

"I will join you too. Your ladies are having far too much fun," Yvonne said excitedly.

"Yvonne, you are most welcome to join us." Jackie jumped into the conversation; it was a good time to promote the cause. "We need to support one another. Grandparents are the glue that holds families together. Most of these poor kids would have ended up in a foster home if it weren't for us. If only the Federal Government could see grandparents in the same way. Foster parents get paid to do the job we are doing, but we don't, and this pisses me off." Jackie's angst was palpable.

"Family benefits and child care subsidies should be attached to children rather than parents. Most of the time, that money is wasted by the biological parent. They get the money, and the kids are not the beneficiaries."

"I agree with you," Tanya said with conviction.

Then Jackie grew more agitated. "If the child subsidy goes directly to the child, that would eliminate the unnecessary financial stress for grandparents. It will help Grandcarers to buy school uniforms. Regardless of who the child lives with, that money should be spent on the child. It's not right that the biological parents can spend that money on booze or drugs. Where is justice, I ask of you?" Her lips thinned before she spoke again. "Do you know, we had to fight for two years just to get a Medicare card, and eventually, after so many attempts at Centrelink, we finally got family benefits for our granddaughter."

"Yeah, but that's no good to me," Tanya responded.

"Why is that?" somebody wanted to know.

"Because I still work, so I don't qualify for any financial help, nothing. Child Care subsidy is means-tested. You have to be on a pension or on the poverty line to get a childcare subsidy. But I still have the identical bills. Raising kids is an expensive business. Who cares about us? We pay tax, subsidising those lazy buggers whose kids we have to look after." Tanya was now quite animated, her hands slicing the air as she concluded, "But if you are employed and earn a decent living, nobody ever gives us anything."

"Yeah. I am in the same boat. Self-funded retirees, we don't exist either. I would have been much better off if I spent my money in casino, rather than wasting it all on lawyers," Donna laughed half-heartedly. The truth of it still hurt.

Yvonne and Rosanne nodded in agreement.

"We can't get any financial support," Yvonne said. "We didn't qualify for Legal Aid because we were still working. We spend a small fortune on lawyers too, but we got nothing much in return."

"Raising three small children is an expensive business. It's not just, is it?" Rosanne said disappointedly.

"Jackie, what happened on your last family court appearance?" Donna asked.

"Nothing much, except more bills from my lawyers. It's

always the same," Jackie huffed at the reality of it. "The conference was all geared up to reconnect Hannah with her mother, pushing and pulling any which way they could towards the biological mother, *my* daughter, who refused to have a drug test. Regardless of that, she wanted more visitation rights.

"Of course, David and I didn't agree. Everything is working towards softening us to agree to let Hannah spend unsupervised time with her mother."

Then Jackie paused … and heaved a breath.

"Would you believe the audacity of the Independent Children's Lawyer when she phoned Hannah and tried to convince her to spend Christmas with her mother? … Well, we objected to that, but at the Family court conference, nobody listened to our concerns. Our own daughter is not fit enough to have unsupervised access. She lives with another low-life boyfriend, which is a bad combination and not a safe home for our granddaughter. But our concerns were dismissed. Instead, they treated us with contempt, making us feel like two stubborn old farts.

"We are not very popular, and seen as being unreasonable, but I don't care. I don't want Hannah to stay with her mother unless she produces a drug test and agrees to get rehabilitated. I am not giving up on my granddaughter, not now, never …

"We are worried sick as Hannah has the right to choose when she turns twelve next year. I pray to God that she will decide to stay with us," Jackie said, her voice faltering with sadness, frustration, and pain.

As she wiped her tears, she asked, "Donna, how are you managing your home situation?"

"We have had a similar experience to you, Jackie. I can indeed empathise with you. After years of wasting time and money at Family Court, we finally accepted consent orders. Isabella's biological mother was given access to see her daughter in consultation with us. But sadly, she has never come to see her daughter.

"I tried to connect with Isabella's maternal grandmother, hoping to build a bridge between us. Isabella's older, maternal half-sister Emma also lives with her paternal grandparents. All of my efforts to reconcile so Isabella can contact her maternal relatives have been unproductive. Isabella's biological mother, Lucy, didn't want to be found. She abandoned Isabella when she was only one year old, and we have never seen her since. Last we heard her boyfriend overdosed and died and that she moved on with another drug supplier. It hurts me deeply that my poor granddaughter will have to deal with the reality that her mother has abandoned her." Donna felt her tears rising too.

"So, what happened with the Family court?" Yvonne asked while everyone else leant further forward to hear.

"We reluctantly agreed to share parental rights with our son Ricky. Family Court wants to keep at least one biological parent in the play. Nobody cared to know that our son has been on a mental disability pension for the past twenty years. We had the limited choice, so we figured it is a better devil you know than a devil you don't.

"The Family Court was unwilling to look at his mental health issues. That is Pandora's Box that nobody wants to look at. It didn't take long, but a decision to share parental rights with our son came back to bite us. The daily struggle to battle with irrational and difficult to deal with mentally ill person is a huge struggle and demands an enormous patience and compromises. Fighting with the hidden devil within a mentally ill person, it's an emotional rollercoaster. Just when you think things will get better, you get pulled back to that dark side.

"And when you think you made some progress, the never-ending saga starts all over again, dragging you into that black hole. Dealing with mental illness is an endless struggle. You never ever win. Fighting that hidden devil is like being in Dante's Hell. Or, more like the punishment of Sisyphus."

"Who is Sisyphus?" Tanya asked, frowning.

"In ancient Greek mythology, Sisyphus was a king. He was punished by Zeus for some misdeed and was forced to roll a huge rock up a hill, only for it to roll down every time it neared the top; he had to repeat this futile action forever. Just like us, fighting an uphill battle when it comes to saving our grandchildren from their irresponsible parents …"

"Some of us are more familiar with the phrase 'It's like pushing shit uphill."

After that statement, Donna looked up and smiled. "That too," she said, making everyone laugh.

"Oh, Donna, I am so sorry to hear that," Tanya said. "You are always so happy and optimistic. You are the one who always cheers us all up, always joking and putting a smile on all our faces. I had no idea."

"Well, Tanya, my friend, we all have a cross we have to carry. I am like *Paliaggio,* that clown in Italian opera, hiding my pain and sorrow while smiling. Isabella can't see me sad or crying. I must be her role model. Teach her to be resilient.

"That is why I smile. Laughter is the best medicine.

Having a good sense of humour will prolong my life, and I enjoy making you laugh too …" Donna said with a shrug.

"I still can't believe what I see … so many grandparents here. Just turn around. They are everywhere. It is amazing to see so many of them. Some of these grandparents are having a much harder life than me so I can't complain."

Tanya nodded. "Seeing so many grandparents in one place is a revelation. So many elderly people should now be able to enjoy their retirement. Still, instead, they have to learn to become parents all over again. I am absolutely amazed at how some of those elderly grandparents can take care of their grandchildren."

"It is nice to see some men coming along, too. Mostly we think of grandmothers, but there are so many men who are helping out with grandkids," someone at the end of the table remarked.

"Yes, it is. My poor husband David has put up with a lot. He has been a pillar of strength to me. It's just unbelievable, but nobody knows we even exist. We should get t-shirts made that say: 'We are the invisible lot'." Jackie laughed.

"… with a picture of a wrinkly with a walking stick pushing a pram," someone else added, stirring up a chuckle in the group.

"No … no …" someone else cut in. "An oldie with a baby car seat on a zimmer frame." That brought a louder laugh.

But the farcical image was too close to the truth for Jackie. She turned and gazed across the centre and sighed. "Just look at poor Ruth. This time, she came with her husband."

Everybody turned around to where Jackie was looking.

"Ruth has nursed her husband for nearly two years. Bruce got really sick. He has stage four prostate cancer and has just finished his chemotherapy."

"I thought it was Ruth who was sick," someone at the table said.

"Oh yes, last year it was. Ruth had a hip replacement. It's good to see her now walking without support."

"How does she manage? I am not sixty yet, and I get exhausted looking after three kids. Being sick, it must have been tough." Rosanne this time.

"Yeah! So many grey heads in one place. I finally realised that I was not alone in raising Isabella. Look at some of these grandparents. They have two or three kids under their care."

"Yeah," Jackie added. "We are lucky we only have one to take care of. I feel so sorry for these poor grandparents who had two or three to raise."

Tanya turned around to get everybody's attention. "It is sad to see what some of these grandparents have gone through. But look around. They are still smiling."

"Some of these grandparents have had support from DCP, so the kids get placed with other family members or foster homes," Jackie responded. "But not me. I don't want anybody telling me how to raise my granddaughter."

When the organisers started making speeches and wishing everyone a happy and prosperous new year, total silence fell across the cafeteria. Then the WANSLEA director announced that Grandparent carers would get a $1,000.00. The WA government honoured their promise to give a bonus present just before Christmas, and instantaneous applause erupted across the venue.

Yvonne, a new member, said enthusiastically, "Hooray! I will get some money too. I've got so many presents on laybys … the extra cash will come in handy."

"Don't get too excited," Jackie cut in sarcastically. "They have to sweeten us up. New Federal elections must be just around the corner. Besides, this is only a once a year payment from the WA government. You won't get anything else from the Federal Government, that's for sure."

"I don't care who it's from. Once a year is better than none at all. Besides, I am not alone – I have met so many lovely ladies like all of you," Yvonne said, still happy.

"I am sure that all the grandparents, like us, are grateful to the WA government for receiving additional financial help, especially arriving just before Christmas. It will help many grandparents struggling around this time of the year," Rosanne confirmed the sentiment everybody was feeling.

Donna was happy, too, and agreed with Rosanne.

Tanya eventually smiled too. "It is good news. I am not greedy. One payment per year is better than none, and it is not means-tested, so I will get it too," she said, smiling. " I will concede … the WA government has finally recognised grandparent carers who are not yet of retirement age and who are still working and paying our taxes."

"Working grandparents have identical bills to us. I also appreciate getting a little support from the state government. I know it is not much, but it will help with school and sporting fees," Donna responded happily.

Jackie smiled and cast her gaze around the group. "Yes, it will help, but I still believe that we should get paid the same as the Foster parents do. They are paid every fortnight. We only get one payment per year."

"Oh, stop it, Jackie! You are always so negative. Don't be so ungrateful. *One* day we may be recognised and get paid like foster parents do." This came from Tanya.

But Jackie just looked at her and shook her head. "Tanya, you are so naïve. We will never be recognised like foster parents. It will cost the Federal Government far too much. Just look at how many grandparents turned out today. There are eighteen thousand of us, in WA alone. Can you imagine how many grandparent carers are all over Australia? And the problem is only going to get much worse. I still volunteer as a counsellor with families with mental illness, domestic violence … and drugs are on the rise. I bet you after Covid-19 is finished with us, there will be many more families that will fall apart. Divorce and separation these days is easy, and the grandparents get stuck babysitting their kids." Jackie raised her hands above her head and laughed. "We, grandparents, are on the bottom of the list for Federal Government funding," she concluded.

"Stop bickering, Jackie. We must take one day at a time. And you agree that today was a good day." Donna remained cheerful, her glass half full. "You all know as well as I do we will continue to look after our children for free because we love them. It is as simple as that. Getting one-of annual payment is a bonus and the icing on the cake."

And everyone agreed with her.

The end-of-year party at that Sci-Tech evening was an excellent experience for everyone. The children had run around, hardly recognisable under all that face paint. Some of the younger ones were exhausted and ready to sleep. As the party wound up, the grandparent carers gathered their children and wished everyone a happy, healthy and safe

New Year for 2022 and beyond. Some of them exchanged phone numbers, promising to meet at the beach again during the school holidays.

On the way home, everyone stayed cheerful. Jackie had won the door prize, which was the highlight of her day. The huge Christmas hamper full of food – decorative ham, chocolates, Christmas pudding and other perishable foods – sat in the back of the van. The atmosphere in the back seat was rowdy, and, as usual, Jackie had the final word when she jokingly said:

"That is the first time I have ever won anything. What a surprise – that hamper is huge. I will donate it to the Salvation Army. Some other poor bugger might need it more than I do. We are going to Margaret River for the Christmas holidays with my sister and her family. She has enough money, so the hamper will make some poor and disadvantaged families happy this Christmas." Jackie smiled, and Donna smiled in her heart.

The mood among friends was joyful. Everybody knew Jackie had a big mouth, but she had a much bigger heart. She would help anybody in need. The children chatted too as they unwrapped their presents though some were so exhausted they had fallen asleep in the van on the way home.

It was such a perfect day for all the Grandcarers. It bonded their friendship as they started talking about the upcoming Christmas preparations, exchanging ideas for activities to celebrate the next festive seasons, and they remained determined that not even Covid-19 restrictions would spoil their fun with their beloved grandkids.

Recycling Christmas gifts

Another year flew by, and the time for the end-of-year celebration came along. This year, Elizabeth volunteered to be the Christmas party host.

Elisabeth had joined the Arts Centre to make some new friends. She loved pottery, and she made a few original pieces that decorated her garden. Although Elizabeth had no children, she embraced the many grandparents she met at the Arts Centre and welcomed them to her enormous home, which was built for entertaining and elaborate parties.

Sadly, when her husband passed away, the money quickly dried up. He had loved to gamble, and she was shocked to find out that he owned a lot of money. After all his outstanding loans had been paid, her exotic lifestyle ended abruptly.

She had been a model at Harrods in London and worked as a designer for some famous fashion houses in her younger years. When she settled in Perth, she had become one of the biggest distributors of French beauty products. Donna had first met Elizabeth at the Myers store in Fremantle when Elizabeth was promoting new and exclusive face products. *Buy one product and get a free facial massage and mask.* Donna still remembers her soft hands as she had stroked and massaged her face, placing a calm mask on her skin that had rejuvenated her tired face.

Donna became a regular client, and their friendship grew

during Fremantle's America's Cup. Her husband was a long-term member of the Fremantle Yacht club and had friends in high places and the best viewing platform to watch all the sailing events. The America's Cup was the most exciting time when the prestigious Cup had gone to another country for the first time in a hundred years.

In the early eighties, Fremantle was a sleepy fishing town, but The America's Cup awakened the sleeping dragon, ignited the people's spirits, and the city came alive. Fremantle was a melting pot where so many cultures blended in harmony and peace.

Suddenly, overnight, Fremantle became a dot on the world map. Everybody wanted to jump on board to celebrate and contribute to building a new city and being part of a vibrant and prosperous future. Alfresco dining, wine, and small family-owned restaurants popped up on every corner of tiny streets. The main street restaurant buzzed with excitement. Market places expanded; live music, festivals, events, and street arts were abundant. The cappuccino strip was busy day and night. People sat at street-corner cafes sipping espresso. The aroma of roasted coffee beans or freshly baked pizza in the outdoor Il-Forno ovens wafted in the air. Donna would close her eyes for a moment or two and be transported back to any small town in the Mediterranean or a small village in Italy or the Croatian islands.

And in this time, her friendship with Elizabeth blossomed.

*****

The grandparents were excited, knowing that Elisabeth

would once again surprise them with her catering skills. All they had to bring was a plate of food to share. Her home was easy to find; it was the biggest house on that street. The entrance, double-glazed pinewood carved doors, led to a spacious hall with marble tiles. The spacious living area, decorated in elegant wallpaper, elaborate leather furniture and silk curtains, connected to the kitchen, then via open French doors to the outdoor area.

The gardens were lush with a huge water fountain encircled by immaculately kept shrubs, camellias, and roses blooming in every colour. The outdoor furniture was just as elaborate. The cane glass table setting for ten was decorated in festive colours.

Every seat had a small gift delicately wrapped in gold and silver bows, and Christmas bonbons were so large and ornate that they covered the entire plate.

As soon as the women sat down, Elizabeth brought out a non-alcoholic champagne fruit punch. The table setting was now cluttered with food and small gifts for each other to share.

Penny was the first to pop bonbons, and the rest followed to find inside little quiz papers.

Valerie stopped. "I am not popping it up. Can I take my bonbons home to my grandson? Justin has never seen such luxurious bonbons."

"Don't worry, Valerie, I've got another box, so you can take a few home," Elisabeth responded with a smile.

"Me too?"

"And me. Can I take a few homes to show off with my friends?" The ladies spoke in unison.

"Yes, of course, you can," Elizabeth reassured them.

Anne couldn't wait and opened some of her small presents. During the Arts and Craft Centre year, the grandparents had made many handmade gifts of pottery, decorative Christmas cards, and shiny ornamental gifts to decorate Christmas trees.

After opening each other presents, they all cheered happily, popped bonbons and wished each other a good and prosperous year to come.

Jenny and Elisabeth had a glass of champagne as some women started telling jokes and laughing.

Valerie, always the biggest joker in the group, was cheerful and happy. She looked gorgeous in her new floral pink dress and white sneakers. Sipping on her fruit punch, she stood up, put her hands on her ample hips and sought some sort of approval.

"Ladies," she started, turning around for all to see, "what do you think of my new dress? I spent days looking around. Good Sammy's. "This was the only dress I could find with elastic in it; it feels so comfortable. Look at me …" She pointed at her tummy. "It feels great. I can breathe much easier now."

"But you changed your hair to pink now. Why is that?" Penny asked.

"It's spray-on colour; it will wash out, but it looks fantastic. I'm still competing with the younger mums. The sandals cost more, but I like to feel comfortable. Summer is the best time to get dressed. It doesn't cost much.

"Look at it, ladies. I even got a new tattoo, a tiny redback spider at the back of my neck. Isn't it super cool?"

"You look fabulous, Valerie." Approvals came from all around the table.

"You look stunning, Valerie. But what news do you have to share with us?"

"Oh yes … Last week, Justin was so happy because he earned $80.00; he was boasting about how smart he is. He started going around the neighbourhood, collecting empty cans and plastic bottles for recycling. He is so enthusiastic about how much money he has already saved for his new bike.

"There's still a few more weeks before Christmas, so Justin and I may make another hundred bucks. It will come in handy to pay off some of my laybys at K-Mart. Luckily, I've made so many Christmas presents at the Arts and Craft Centre, so I won't have to spend so much this year."

"Wow, it is good to hear that Justin is earning some money," Penny commented.

"I believe it's good that Justin has a new hobby. Now all the neighbours are leaving so many bottles and cans on my front porch. When Justin comes home from school, he busily sorts it all out. This is doubly great because it has kept him away from his iPad. Last week, I drove Jason to the recycling place. My car boot was full of bottles and beer cans. It took them more than an hour to count it all up. I got sick of waiting, so I went inside to hurry things up. The young man there told me it would be quicker to go online.

"As you know, I've got a bit of a hearing problem, so I gave this young man a piece of my mind. 'Don't be a silly, young man. I've got my washing on line. I like to get cash in my hands, to touch and smell my money. Just give us the cash, so we can go home."

Valerie was on a roll. "Ladies, as far as I am concerned, on-line is for washing. Net is for fishing. Web is for spiders.

By the way, my trusty old Hills Hoist washing line is still standing and full of spiders. I can't afford to get Pest Control in as I don't have any spare cash."

The group of ladies couldn't get a word in, as Valerie kept rabbiting on. "We never had much cash around, anyway. My husband is so stingy; he wouldn't put his hands in his pocket, it's as if it was full of spiders. Eventually, he tired of living with an old person like me, so he traded me in for a newer model – found himself an online bride from the Philippines. He took the savings and his credit cards with him and left for good. I can't get a credit card in my name because I don't have credit ratings. I suppose I must be too old …

"Anyway, I told this young man, 'Listen, mate, I don't have a line of credit so there's no point sending it to the bank. I need money right now to put some petrol in my car. I work with cash only.' But I don't think he really cared. He gave me the money just to get rid of me." Valerie laughed at herself.

"We aren't much better off with all that technology. My Justin used to spend all day on YouTube or his iPad. Now that Justin is collecting and recycling, he gets much more exercise. While walking around the neighbourhood, some of his friends have joined him too. Fresh air will do them all good."

Penny shook her head. "All these modern gadgets are no good; kids are now spoiled more than ever. Parents are so busy that they use tablets as a babysitting tool. I applaud you, Valerie, for making Justin earn his pocket money."

But Valerie hadn't finished her story. "What's the world coming to," she said. "These days, everybody is using plastic cards. No more personal service. We have to scan our groceries too. It would be much better if our grandkids got some casual work instead."

Then Anne lifted her glass and tapped it with a fork to get everybody's attention. "Kids should play in the park with other kids like we used to. When my grandson Oliver gets older, we will start collecting recyclables. It will be a moral lesson for Oliver to earn his own pocket money too."

"I wish to God recycling was popular when my husband Joe was alive."

"Why's that?" Jenny asked.

"Well, my husband was drunk most of the time and would torment the kids and me. He was such a pisspot … sitting all day on a couch like a fat, worthless blob, holding on to his beer cans, and drinking until he passed out."

She stopped for a moment and laughed. "Ladies, could you only imagine. If I had started collecting Joe's beer cans while he was still alive, I could have stacked his empty cans to be as tall as the Empire State Building. Gee, if recycling was popular in those days, I'd be a millionaire by now. Instead, I spent a small fortune paying for his funeral insurance, praying and hoping that alcohol would help bury him sooner rather than later. But the old bastard lived forever and ruined everybody else's lives."

As the club treasurer, Penny stood up to gain the group's attention. "Good on you, Valerie. It's good to hear that kids are earning their pocket money. Kids should be taught to respect money. It doesn't grow on trees," she concluded.

Typical of Penny, she is always so rational when it comes to money, Donna thought.

"Yes." Elisabeth nodded. "Recycling is good. I recycle

everything and make my compost too."

"Wow! That is why your garden looks so good."

"So what's been happening in your life, Jenny?" Anne asked.

Jenny smiled. "I've been working for a while now, cleaning a pub on an early shift so I could get home before the girls go to school. And ladies, have I got a recycling story to tell you … but be prepared.

Valerie's eyebrow rose and a cautious look crossed her face. She knew Jenny well. "Prepared for what?" she asked hesitantly.

"When I finally got enough courage to date again," Jenny started, "I was so happy that I had found the man of my dreams. I felt young enough, and my fire was still burning. When I met Trevor, I fell head over heels in love with him. Everything was going fine … until he started cheating. Trevor didn't want to have any baggage at home. I suppose he didn't want to hang around with somebody of my age." She pulled a face. "My girls still need me, and Trevor didn't want an instant family. I told him that my girls are now at high school and easy to look after. However, he got cold feet and skipped town." Then she laughed.

"What's so funny?" Valerie asked, still wary of what was coming.

"No man would want to get serious with a woman of my age, especially one who is looking after two teenagers. I turned sixty, so I'm not a young chick anymore."

"Don't be silly, Jenny! You look so sexy. You are still young, so don't give up. You'll find somebody else. Not all men are the same? And being with mature women has its rewards.

"Such as?" Jenny giggled. "Don't be silly, Valerie. Men only want one thing … or two."

"What's that?" Anne asked.

"Young girls with firm bottoms to warm his bed, and us old chooks to cook his meals. That's it.

"I don't want to date anybody soon. Men are nothing but trouble. And I certainly don't want to cook or clean up after them or share my bed until they find other younger women.

"I got so depressed when I found out that Trevor had got himself a younger woman, one half his age. I tell you, ladies, keep the man happy in bed and feed him well. That's all that it takes. When the man turns sixty, he is classified as sophisticated and charming. When a woman turns sixty, she is called an old bag."

Everybody laughed, considering she was right on the mark.

"And guess what, ladies … I'll be taking the girls down south soon. Fortune has smiled on me." She smiled wryly. "Some unexpected money came my way."

"Yeah?" Penny prompted.

"The other day when I was cleaning and throwing out all of Trevor's junk that he left behind, a golf ball rolled out of the closet and next to my foot. When I bent down to pick it up, I spotted his expensive golf clubs under a jacket that had fallen off a hanger. He had obviously missed seeing it when he packed. Anyway, I checked out the leather bag and gold stick holder and found a receipt in it. Wow!! It was one of those gold tournament buggy slips. The golf package was some sort of expensive brand which must have cost him a small fortune.

That same afternoon, my friend Brenda came over and I

told her how expensive Trevor's golf clubs are. She laughed, telling me we should put it on eBay and sell it. I wasn't keen to do that because Trevor really liked golf, but Brenda convinced me it was a good way to get even with that cheating bastard."

"What did you do?" Everybody wanted to know.

"Sold it, of course. I got two thousand dollars for it. I told the girls I will take them to Margaret River to watch the surfing competition."

"What did you tell Trevor?"

"He called to make arrangements to pick them up, and I left him a message that his golf clubs had gone on a surfing trip. He started to make a fuss about that so I told him to consider it as overdue rent! I suppose he figured that was a small price to pay for his cheating and walking out on me and I didn't hear from him again."

Everyone raised their glasses in a toast to Jenny and settled back to think and smile about her audacity.

"Have you done your Christmas shopping?" Elizabeth asked Penny, changing the subject.

Penny sighed with pleasure. "Yes, I'm all organised. At the Art and Crafts group, we have made enough presents to go around for our kids and family. For Grandcarers, time and money are precious commodities. Grandparents sacrifice a lot to save some money so their grandkids will have presents under the Christmas tree."

Olivia felt quite proud of herself, telling everyone, "I got all the presents done months in advance."

"What's your secret?" they all asked in awe.

"Well, during the year, I chase all the red light specials, buying a little every month. You'd be surprised how many new things you will find in Salvos. Obviously, some parents buy presents the kids don't want, and some of them end up donated, still with their original wrapping and stickers on. By the time Christmas comes around, I have everything done. I also rely on a charity organisation that offers food hampers for people who are struggling financially. Every year I put my name down so I don't miss out."

"That's just what Grandcarers have to do. No kids should miss out on turkey and ham for Christmas," Penny affirmed. "It's a lucky country for some, but not for most of us Grandcarers," she added.

Olivia looked around the table before she spoke again. "I re-gift as much as possible … you know, things that I don't like or don't need. I recycle presents; just change the stickers and use last year's recycled wrapping paper. I throw nothing away. But I got caught a few times, re-gifting to the same person. That was embarrassing, but I am more careful now.

"Ladies, gee, I hope I didn't give anybody a gift that I received from you at our last Christmas party." She giggled apologetically, but nobody would have cared anyway.

Maureen, at seventy, had been a single mother for years. She had already raised her own kids, and her grandchildren, too, and had learnt most of the tricks of managing.

"I did my Christmas shopping last year," she said proudly. "I shop all year round, looking for specials, mostly practical presents, stationery, books, clothes and shoes. I've made all my Christmas cards from recycled cards at the Arts and Craft group and I recycle all my Christmas wrapping paper too.

"For all of my extended family, friends and neighbours, every year I make a special Christmas cake, made from walnuts, almonds, dry fruits, and a good drop or two of brandy to make it last for a few weeks.

"In return, they buy me things that my grandkids need. That helps me a lot too."

Maureen beamed when everyone wanted to have her cake recipe. Elisabeth turned around and proudly showed off the Christmas cake Maureen had made for her.

"I am not sharing it with anybody. It's all mine," she smiled. "I have it every night with my cup of tea."

"So how many years have you each been looking after your grandkids?" Elisabeth was keen to know.

Maureen had the answers that most grandparents agreed with. "We always hoped that our adult children would eventually take over as responsible parents. I waited for over twenty years, then my husband got sick of waiting, and died. But I'm still around, taking care of my great-grandchildren now. And I have to be around for a few more years at least to see them grow up.

"My oldest granddaughter, Becky, got married and had twin girls. Her partner was extremely violent, and she got a restraining order against him and moved back in with me. She's working, and I am at home looking after her two kids. Hollie, my youngest granddaughter, is studying a TAFE. She's a good girl. I am struggling to pay for her tuition fees and books, and she likes to wear fashionable clothes now, but I just can afford to buy them for her."

Maureen continued. "A friend of mine has two teenage kids living with her. This year DCP arranged that her grandkids should spend Christmas with their mum in Kalgoorlie. When the kids turn sixteen, they can choose who they want to live with. It's difficult enough to let go, but that was bad timing as nobody should be alone for Christmas. I invited Betty to have lunch with us as my house is always full of kids so she will feel at home. I made her one of my cakes too." She smiled. "Put enough brandy in it and it will solve anyone's problems."

She chuckled and continued with her story. "I understand how it feels to be alone. I did something just for myself this year – I joined a bowling club. I needed somewhere to get some peace away from the noisy kids. I figured that playing with that silly ball on the lawns is not that hard. I went out a few times to bingo night and dancing, too, but I quit because those old people were so dull. I realised I preferred to stay home with my grandkids. They are much more fun to be around, and they keep me young, too." Maureen's eyes sparkled at the warm images her words brought. "Besides," she added, "it is much better hanging around you ladies. I love coming to the Arts and Crafts meetings. We have such a good laugh together, don't we?"

"God knows it is better to laugh than cry about some of these silly anecdotes we grandparents have shared with one another," Penny summed it all up.

The Christmas party drew to an end, some grandmothers having to rush off to be home for their grandkids. Donna went to the kitchen and started helping Elizabeth pack leftover lunch for everybody to take home. All the boxes were immaculately packed, including decorative cups that Elizabeth had made in her pottery class, with a few bonbons and cards made from recycling old Christmas cards.

*****

Donna didn't see many grandparents during school

holidays, but the Dog Club was always alive and vibrant with noise and play. Some of the grandparents continued to socialise together more often and went camping with their grandkids, travelling together in groups to share the costs of chalets or cabins, which was safer and cheaper. God knew they needed a holiday, as most of these ladies have given the best parts of their lives to their grandkids. They could all do with a few weeks' rest.

Donna didn't see them often, but she knew how resourceful they all were in managing their lives the best way they knew how. She knew it was not up to her to judge their lifestyles or their survival methods and admired them all for their tenacity.

She thought: *if an outsider who is not familiar with the grandparents' plights could be a fly on the wall and listen to some conversations going on, although, quite tragic, it would be most amusing … hilarious.*

*****

A few weeks later, Tanya called to say that she had planned with some of their old work colleagues to meet for lunch at the foreshore. It was apparent that her work colleagues were complaining much more about their lives and their grandchildren. They seemed so focused on themselves, some wanting sympathy and bitching about everything and nothing. They were preoccupied with their careers, with not having any financial problems, with planning their overseas holidays.

Their parenthood was all but gone, and their grandchildren were Christmas decorations, only having them around for a while, and giving them back as soon the festive season was over. God forbid, they couldn't be an interruption to their so-called normal lives.

"I love and spoil my grandkids for two or three days, then handle them back to their parents," most of them would say.

On that day on the Boardwalk, the group of eight ladies Donna had worked with before her retirement caught up on work gossip. This included which department was in favour, or not; who got promoted and why and who got sacked; who was ill, and how many pills they were taking; what kind of pain medicine or antidepressants they were taking to cope with the stressful work environment.

Patricia said to Kerry, "I've been so depressed lately, so I am getting some counselling to cope better as the workload is overwhelming. I get so annoyed when my daughter brings her two kids on the weekend. I told her I was not here as her free babysitter. I can't be bothered with all those screaming kids, especially during school holidays. That time is strictly for me."

Kerry agreed. "Oh yes, kids are a pain in the proverbial you know what. During school holidays, I have them over a few times at my place, but I get so tired because they want so much attention. I don't have any peace to read a book or spend time with my partner."

Robyn added fuel to the conversation. "When I have my grandkids with me, I don't have time to go to the gym; I miss my daily workout; I go at least once or twice to yoga, it's so relaxing it takes all the stress away. When my grandkids come for a visit, I have to cook nuggets and pizzas and put all that weight on. After Christmas, I have to go back to dieting. Nothing fits me anymore," she said, looking at her slightly round belly.

"What have you been doing, Simone? Are you still working as an enrolment officer?" Donna asked.

"Oh, yeah, end-of-year is so hectic. I had to deal with disgruntled parents and grandparents. Most of them want to pay their fees in instalments and some don't make their payments on time. I get so fed up with sending letters reminding them that if they don't pay on time, they can re-enrol. It annoys me. Why can't people pay the bills like the rest of us do? I dread next semester's enrolment as there will be so many outstanding fees for me to deal with."

Kelsie, who worked in the Vocational Education Training Section, had to visit schools and organise work experience for students who had completed all the theory components. "Covid-19 shutdowns have disrupted some of their practical training," Kelsie complained. "I have no choice but to continue working, and I'm fed up with dealing with students. It isn't enjoyable because they can't complete their practical training. I had to postpone all my on-the-job assessments. I am so sick of all these shutdowns. It will have so much extra work when we go back. But I told my boss that I was taking some time off work as stress leave."

Tanya shook her head. "What happened, Roslyn. Why are you taking so many painkillers?"

"During the winter holiday, we went to New Zealand. I had a go at bungee jumping. That was always on my bucket list. I must have dislocated my back, and I have been in continuous pain ever since. And migraines. My back pain drives me crazy. Then my son expects me to look after his kids during the school holidays. I told him I won't be able to have them around my place as often, and he got so mad and stormed out of my house. He's so selfish and doesn't think about how I feel."

"Yeah, I agree with you," Donna said. "Most of our kids are like that. Let me tell you about ..." but she stopped and thought, *Nancy and this group will never understand grandparent carers' life-long struggles. There's no point in saying anything.*

Nancy had a sip of her wine, waiting, then continued her story about holiday plans when Donna remained silent.

"We started planning a cruise to the Mediterranean coast, but the bloody Covid-19 ruined our plans. I only hope that it won't last much longer. Frankly, I am sick and tired of all these lock-downs. My husband is impatient; he was looking forward to that cruise."

Rene, the youngest staff member in the group, was applying her lipstick, turning around to get some more compliments. Donna remembered that when they worked together, Rene was a hypochondriac. If she was not stressed due to work schedules, she was sick. She was vain, and hated the idea of getting older. As she finished her make-up touch up, she said, "Ladies, did you notice I had my boobs done?" She was not wearing a bra.

"I had my operation done in Thailand as it was cheaper. But when I got home, one of my boobs was leaking. I needed another new procedure to rectify the problem. But I feel much more confident now as I can wear my bikinis again. As soon as this locked down is over, I will go back to Bali. My son went on a surfing holiday there, met a girl, and now he has a kid. He wanted to bring her back to Perth, but I told them he could stay with her in Bali. I would come and visit them instead.

"Like the rest of you, I am too young to be a grandmother. I just couldn't stand having little kids around me. I suppose that makes me selfish, but I don't care. I finish my parenting, and if my son wants to have kids, he can take care of them because I certainly won't."

Donna looked at Rene harshly. *She's not changed one bit. The entire world revolves around her. It is all about Rene,* she thought. Then she felt surprised. Her work colleagues were so self-absorbed, living in their own bubble. *A tiny world indeed,* she observed. *I can't believe I never noticed that before, but this is an eye-opener.*

She could not believe how much time they had wasted on negative talk about who was taking more pills, like it was competing in some sort of sports competition, and endlessly complaining about COVID-19 shutdowns because they couldn't travel overseas.

She nodded sadly. These people couldn't even notice a long sandy beach with blue skies and endless horizons and see the beautiful surroundings all around the foreshore. As she sat back, sipping her glass of wine, observing and admiring the view, she thought of Maureen and the other grandmothers. *These self-absorbed people live in a bubble of their own choosing. They don't even know that Grandcarers exist. What would they know about stress, sleepless nights, nappies, playing games, and volunteering at a Day-Care or school extracurricular activities? They would have no time to be depressed. Grandcarers cope with migraines or headaches in silence. Taking care of their grandchildren comes above anything else.*

She looked at these women critically and realised that, when she was employed, she was ignorant too. She looked further around the table, thinking herself lucky that she'd kept her sunglasses on as she scrutinised one woman after another. *How much they have all aged,* crossed her mind. It made her feel old just to be around them. *They live in a different world or universe.*

Donna looked at Tanya, and both said almost in unison: "Ladies, we'd love to chat longer, but we have to pick up our grandchildren from school and take them to swimming lessons."

While exchanging farewell pleasantries and waving goodbye, Donna couldn't help herself. "Ladies, looks like COVID-19 may hang around longer than we think. Why don't you think about having a holiday right here in WA where we are all safe? So much to see. Just look around; we live in the best part of the world. Why would you want to go anywhere else?" She swept her hands out towards the vast Indian Ocean.

"Just look at the beautiful sandy beaches, blue skies, and family-friendly town safe for kids to play. The entire world is envious of our freedom to travel, have fun and be safe, too. WA has so much to offer. It has everything. You are looking at it but not seeing it. Why would you want to go anywhere else?"

"Bye for now," and Donna and Tanya waved as they made their escape.

Walking to the bus stop together, they looked at each other, smiling.

"This lunch was a waste of our valuable time," Tanya complained.

Donna nodded. "Yeah, but it was an eye-opener too. Ciao, Bella. See you next week at the doggy beach."

On the way home, Donna finally realised that she didn't miss her old colleagues anymore. Being retired had its rewards: she had made so many new friends that she really liked. And she didn't miss her work anymore. She was free – the only thing she missed was the loss of her income.

On arriving home, she made a cup of coffee and joined Tom on the balcony.

"How was your lunch with colleagues?" he asked.

She shook her head. "Tom, I can't believe that when I worked with these people, I had blinkers on. It is like I lived on another planet."

"Don't be so hard on yourself. You didn't know any better back then, but now you do."

She shook her head again, almost lost for words. "I cannot believe they are all so self-centred, talking about their problems. I wish they can all walk in a Grandcarer's shoes for a while. They might learn about the world. Grandcarers don't have time to feel depressed, stressed, or sick. They just keep making sacrifices for the benefit of the next generation of children. They are the glue that keeps families together."

She wanted to give the voices to so many grandparents, the invisible ones who, to her, were the unsung heroes.

From that day on, she referred to them as "The Silent Heroines."

COVID-19 – The New Normal

Penny, the Arts and Crafts treasurer, was always full of big ideas, and an end of the year on the beach with grandparents and their kids was one of these perfect ideas.

Arriving at the beach early, she ensured the grandmothers and their grandkids got the best spot by reserving an area close to the playground and a drinking fountain.

Every child was to receive a small Christmas gift, and Penny had started shopping for gifts months in advance, looking for special deals, buying gifts that had a practical use, such as beach towels, sunscreens or water bottles, pencils, crayons, and toddler buckets and spades for building sandcastles.

Donna had assisted by securing a donation of children's books written by local authors, from the local book club and other writing organisations.

It was a perfect day at the beginning of summer, a lovely time for all the grandparents to relax and not to have any worries, a day they could sit on their recliner chairs, chat, and enjoy the sunshine.

Setting up early was essential to get the best spot, under the shade of big pine, firs and eucalyptus trees. Summer made the oil in the leaves smell so fresh, and birds flew and fed chicks, chirping melodically and entertaining anyone who wanted to listen. Yellow-tailed parrots hung upside down on fragile branches, performing acrobatic maneuvers, looking like they would fall but surprising everyone when they dropped gracefully to the ground. Tiny blue-breasted finches joined in, flapping their wings so fast as they raced each other to reach the tallest spot on the enormous pine trees on the foreshore.

Picnics spots filled fast as people unpacked their chairs and picnic tables. Kids lay on the picnic blankets in their bathers or wrapped themselves in extra-large beach towels while mums tried to apply sunscreen. Dads and granddads gathered around the barbecue ready to cook sausages, chops, and fresh seafood, enjoying a perfect summer day on a perfect beach. Not a cloud marred the sky as kids happily ran free, trying to catch one another.

By lunchtime, the foreshore was full, some having travelled from distant suburbs to spend a day at the best beach in WA. At restaurants, alfresco dining was in full swing, too, full of patrons enjoying a meal or snack as a light breeze carried the smell of freshly brewed espresso coffee.

The mouth-watering smell of fish and chips from across the road made everyone hungry and was always a special occasion for Grandcarers and kids. No washing up was a bonus, and leftovers of chips attracted seagulls that the children chased up the beach.

Although most kids could swim, grandmothers took turns to sit on the sand dunes under the umbrella, posing as an unofficial coast guard armed with a spray bottle of vinegar just in case the blue bottle jellyfish came in. The safety of their grandkids was always important to observe. Observing kids' activities from a safe distance allowed them to play freely. And indeed, they ran in and out of the water, jumped, pushed one another, chased waves, and threw Frisbees. The smaller kids immersed themselves in digging a big hole and building sandcastles.

"Come on, ladies, let's go for a swim. Who is going to relieve Jenny? She must be sick of sitting there all on her own."

"I'll go," Gail offered as she helped Donna up off her towel.

Donna looked around. "Come on, Izzy, I'll chase you," she said. "Let's see who will get to swim first."

Little Izzy splashed into the waves first. Donna was not far behind …

*****

The end year soon approached, but the coronavirus was here to stay. And they all altered their lives accordingly, learning to adjust to this new normality.

Because of the restrictions, everyone had to make some adjustments. Social distancing meant no kids were allowed at many places. Before Covid-19, around Christmas time, Donna always had a house full of kids. Not to disappoint, Isabella and Donna spent hours wrapping small presents in a variety of coloured decorative paper. The day before Christmas, they went to homes in their area, delivering small parcels for Izzy's little friends to be placed under their Christmas trees.

That year, to commemorate the exceptional circumstances of living with Covid-19, Isabella suggested they should buy a brand-new Christmas tree to surprise Santa. So they immersed themselves in decorating a brand-new Christmas tree, carefully unpacking all the delicate ornamental balls from a large plastic container and placing all the decorations on the tree.

When it was done, the tree stood full of colourful glitter, lights, and tinsel. It was such a beautiful, tall Christmas tree. As a finale, Izzy climbed on her grandpa's shoulders and placed an angel on the top of her new tree.

Standing back a few steps, they all admired their new masterpiece. "Wow!" Donna said. "The new tree is so tall. It looks so great. Thanks for helping me with the decorations," she said, scruffing Izzy's hair.

"Nana, the lights on the tree are so pretty, all the colours of the rainbow, so bright Santa will find his way around our house." Izzy clapped her hands excitedly.

"Yes, my sweet. Santa will be really impressed at how skilful you are in placing all the ornaments. The new tree looks so beautiful. Regardless of Covid-19, this Christmas will be extra special. Nothing will stop Santa from delivering presents to all the boys and girls all over the world. But, sweetie, we are fortunate to be living in WA, as this is the safest place to be."

"Nana, Santa will be really happy because he doesn't have to wear a mask so he can eat his cookies and milk."

"Yes, my love, you are right. We are all so lucky to be healthy."

"Nana," Isabella asked next, "can you give our old Christmas tree to my friend Lilly? Because of the coronavirus, her stepdad lost his job. Lily told me she won't be able to celebrate Christmas this year. That is so sad, isn't it, Nana?"

"Yes, of course, we can give Lilly our tree. We can give her some decorations, tinsel, and unique lights too."

"Lilly and her baby brother will be so happy. She will at least have a lovely Christmas tree. Can we buy her some toys too, so she has something under her tree before Santa visits?" She looked up at her Nana hopefully.

"Every child deserves to celebrate Christmas," Donna said, nodding, and she bent down and hugged her granddaughter for her generosity.

Izzy squirmed out of her arms and ran across the room. "Let's put the tree into this big plastic box so we can take it to her tomorrow."

"Oh, no, I can't give her that box," Donna gasped.

"But why not? The old Christmas tree fits perfectly." Izzy turned her questioning eyes towards her grandmother.

"Well, my sweet. This box has a special meaning for me. I will never part with it."

"Why? Where did you get this old box?"

Tom smiled indulgently at his inquisitive granddaughter.

Sitting down next to her husband, Donna patted the cushion for Isabella to sit next to her. "Well, let me tell you. When you were a baby, that shallow plastic container served as your first bed. I would pack the box with soft pillows and even softer, cuddly blankets that you loved so much, and you would fall asleep in no time. This box was to stop you from toppling over since we didn't have a cradle. Now and then, we'd bounce you in gentle motions to soothe your baby cries, and your granddad carried you in that container all around the house.

"We loved to see our little angel peacefully sleeping in that special little crèche," she said, gently stroking her fingers through Izzy's curly hair and softly touching her cheek.

"When you got bigger, you started sleeping in a cot. I got so attached to that box and kept our Christmas decoration in it to remind me of you." Donna leaned over a dropped a soft kiss on her cheek.

"Okay, Nana, you can keep the box," Izzy responded. "Bon-Bon can now sleep in it." She put a few soft pillows into the box and started chasing Bon-Bon all around the house, dragging her when she caught her into her new sleeping box.

Izzy was indeed pleased, jumping around the tree, excited that her friend Lilly and her little brother Connor would find Santa's presents under a beautiful, glittering Christmas tree.

Tom and Donna looked up at the innocence of the child. Donna turned around when Tom said, "For Lilly and her family. Covid-19 will not spoil her Christmas. Instead, it will be a memorable and joyful one. I am sure Santa will be pleased too."

That night Izzy slept so peacefully, cuddling Bon-Bon, who later curled up and slept in that same box she had slept in as a baby. Donna's heart was at peace as she sat next to her husband and sighed. Tom looked at her face, knowing what she was thinking, but he didn't want to spoil that perfect moment.

With the Christmas lights illuminating the lounge, Donna turned and said softly, as if scared to utter those few words. "Oh, Tom, I wonder if maybe this Christmas Isabella's mother might come and see her little girl. That would be such a special Christmas."

Tom gently patted Donna's hand to reassure her. "Darling, don't spoil today, just hope that tomorrow will be different. It is time that you come to terms that Isabella's mother will not come this Christmas or the next. So stop wishing. Even Santa can never grant Isabella's wish to reunite with her mother."

"Oh, Tom, Christmas is so special. It might soften her heart …"

"Yeah, baby. You will forever be the eternal optimist. That is why I married you." And he leaned over and gently kissed his wife.

*****

Because of Covid-19, the Christmas pageant was cancelled, but the social distancing restrictions were much more relaxed. All the people in the neighbourhood adjusted their lives slightly. However, it didn't stop them from participating in the summer activities in their accustomed style.

Kids welcomed Santa at the Rockingham Foreshore. "Look, Nana, there's Santa Claus." Isabella pulled Donna's hand to get her attention and pointed up ahead. Indeed, there was Santa – he'd come to town right on time, surprising all the kids who cheered him on.

They spent the day at the beach with Izzy and her friends taking part in fun kids' activities such as fairies, face painting and bouncy castles. Families sang Christmas carols and admired the world's best sunset while exhausted kids enjoyed a meal of fish and chips and ice creams.

That evening the beachfront Christmas lights glittered, so many bright, decorative colours sparkling on the tall pine trees, creating an illusion that connected them with the stars above. As they walked among the rainbow of colours, the joy felt contagious, and with the soothing ocean breeze adding to the celebratory mood, it felt like they had entered an enchanted world.

Isabella and her little friends ended up dancing on the stage with Santa and his elves. As usual, Izzy was the centre of attention, enjoying the day with other carefree kids who just wanted to have fun. When they arrived home that night, they all crashed into bed, totally exhausted. Isabella fell asleep the moment her head hit the pillow.

The lights in their house sparkled during the festive season, glowing brightly and making sure Covid-19 didn't ruin their Christmas festivities or stop Santa from delivering gifts.

The 2021 New Year's Eve fireworks at the foreshore were cancelled because of COVID-19, but who cared anyway. COVID-19 wasn't going to spoil people's enthusiasm. Enjoying dinner at Rockingham Beach, sipping glasses of champagne and marvelling at the sunset was even better. If Covid-19 restrictions were the new normal, then that was a great way to end a tough year.

Time had stood still, a reminder for all to stop and enjoy the finer things in life. Tom and Donna held hands, watching Izzy and Bon-Bon run and play on the beach, chasing waves and seagulls. They walked barefoot on the long sandy beach, amazed at the bright red sky full of sunset colours stretching to the horizon. Later, under a bright full moon and a clear sky full of stars, celebrations continued.

After the Covid-19 lockdown was lifted, people in the neighbourhood gathered together in the little park opposite the lake and had picnics to celebrate any special occasion.

During Covid-19 year, they felt so lucky to welcome two majestic swans landing on their lake.

Tom and Donna sat on the balcony, their favourite place to admire the beauty around them. Donna lifted her glass of wine and looked tenderly at her husband.

"Darling," she said, "aren't we lucky? We are blessed with the good fortunes to be living in the best part of the world."

"Here, here. I agree with that. Today has been a perfect day."

"Yeah. And tomorrow will be another perfect day. God must have chosen this part of the world as his sacred place. He must have kept it as his best holiday destination." Donna smiled back.

"I agree with that too, that's for sure." Tom laughed. "Even God needs a safe place to live. So he comes to WA."

Donna was quiet for a long while. Then she heaved a sigh. "Tom, I have decided when Isabella is older, I will make sure she knows how lucky she is to have had such a privileged and safe life. To have our home right here in Rockingham is such a blessing." Tom nodded in agreement. "I will teach Isabella to appreciate her good fortune, to be grateful for sharing life on this unique yet fragile blue planet. Covid-19 has made us appreciate and cherish our unique place on Earth, and celebrate every day as we make happy memories."

Tom turned to his wife and made his big statement for the night. "Well, my love, if Covid-19 has taught us one moral lesson, it is to recognise just how fragile our life could be. Never take the Australian lifestyle for granted. Not now, not ever."

She nodded. "Our home is a special place under the sun

for all of us to enjoy, and we must celebrate every day as if
it is the last."

THE END

About the Author

Nada Lubay was born in Croatia and, at the tender age of twenty-two, emigrated to Australia. She has lived in Perth, Western Australia, for more than forty years and would never live anywhere else.

Nada had a successful career in Vocational Education Training, working for a Registered Training Organisation (RTO) and was passionate about helping young students, some from dysfunctional family backgrounds. She was instrumental in them gaining employment and becoming productive members of the community.

Nada's life dramatically changed when she left the workforce to raise her infant granddaughter. Battling the court system to secure a safe environment for her granddaughter, she works tirelessly to gain recognition and equal standing for the thousands of grandparent carers who are also raising their grandchildren due to a broken society.

The Silent Heroines is Nada's first novel.

She is currently writing her second novel, *The Silent Tears*, which will be released in early 2023.